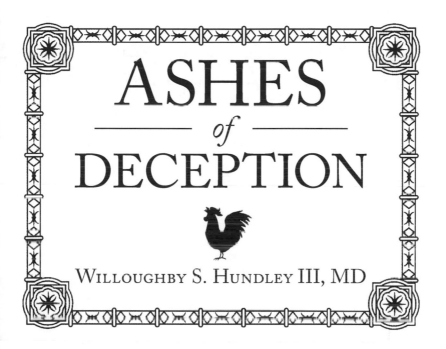

ASHES
of
DECEPTION

Willoughby S. Hundley III, MD

iUniverse, Inc.
Bloomington

Ashes of Deception

iUniverse books may be ordered through booksellers or by contacting:

iUniverse
1663 Liberty Drive
Bloomington, IN 47403
www.iuniverse.com
1-800-Authors (1-800-288-4677)

ISBN: 978-1-4759-5940-6 (sc)
ISBN: 978-1-4759-5942-0 (hc)
ISBN: 978-1-4759-5941-3 (e)

Library of Congress Control Number: 2012921229

Printed in the United States of America

iUniverse rev. date: 11/15/2012

My greatest thanks for the support
and tolerance of my wife, Lucy

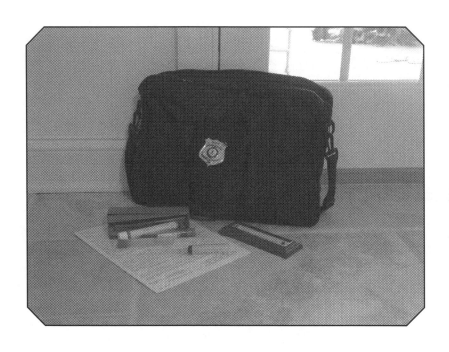

County Medical Examiner | 1

THE BEEP-BEEP-BEEP-BEEP ABRUPTLY WAKENED DR. Obie Hardy from a deep, restful sleep. He fumbled on the bed stand to locate and silence the disturbance. Straining in the dark, he read the digits against the glowing green display on his beeper: 9-1-1. This was not the usual four-digit hospital extension he was accustomed to. The clock displayed 3:10.

"This is Dr. Hardy," he said after calling the emergency number.

"We need a medical examiner," announced the dispatcher.

Obie Hardy groaned. He was one of the six physicians in Mecklenburg County who performed this service. Since he hadn't had a case in two months, he was overdue. He hurriedly put on some khaki pants and a T-shirt and slipped his bare feet into a pair of Topsiders by the back door.

The bitter cold night air slapped him awake as he stepped out of the door and scampered into his chilled Jeep Cherokee. He made a quick stop at his office to retrieve the four-page CME-1 report form, a pen, and a clipboard. The dispatcher had given him a house address, so it wouldn't be a highway fatality. Dr. Hardy expected it would be the routine—an elderly man found dead at home from natural causes, with no recent medical care. But as he traveled down Old Cox Road, the pulsating glow of flashing red and blue lights above the horizon ahead told him that this might be more involved.

An overweight deputy approached the doctor as he closed the driver's door of his Jeep. "The first one's over here," he said, motioning toward the door of a mobile home.

"The first one?" asked Hardy.

"Yeah. A murder-suicide."

Obie Hardy sighed. "I only brought one form." As the frigid February air flowed over his ankles, he wished he had brought some socks as well as a second medical examiner's form.

Anna Thacker lay facing up about twenty feet from the front door of the mobile home. Her eyes were open, eerily staring at the sky. A dark red puddle of blood extended from behind her head, and an open wound was obvious on her right temple. In the center of the blood pool, a pale yellow fragment of bone the size of a quarter caught Obie's eye. He could feel the warmth of her body against the cold night as he placed his thermometer under her right arm. It was a plastic, rectangular outdoor thermometer covered by a ziplock bag. The technique was backwoods-like, but by the time Obie Hardy completed his body survey, he had an axillary temperature reading of 76 degrees to record. In unwitnessed deaths, heat loss charts could help approximate the time of death.

"We figure she was shot about 2:33," stated Johnson, the plump deputy, still standing by Dr. Hardy. "The call came in at 2:35. We were on the scene in eight minutes, at 2:43. Deputy Harris and I found him in the yard, pacing back and forth, shaking his head. We asked him to drop his weapon, and he just stopped and put it to his head. We weren't here two minutes before he shot himself."

Obie began focusing on the second body, Mohammed Thacker. He paced off the distance from the first body as he approached Mohammed, who lay in the opposite corner of the yard. The spotlight from the police cruiser harshly shadowed the body, also facing up, with a vacuous look in his eyes. A handgun was near his outstretched right arm.

"So you witnessed this shooting?"

"Yeah. Me and Wayne Harris."

"Has anyone taken photos?" asked Dr. Hardy.

"Yeah. Investigator Bruce Duffer took 'em. We got plenty." Johnson gestured toward the mobile home. Dr. Hardy saw through the storm glass door the silhouette of an officer with a camera, taking statements from the people inside.

Obie moved the outstretched left arm alongside the torso, putting the bagged thermometer under the dead man's shirt, in the armpit. Now tremulous, Obie's rubber-gloved fingers had become cold and numb in the bitter night. Ink was reluctant to flow from his pen, which was making note-taking awkward. As he leaned over the body, his nose nearly dripped water from the cold air; he sniffed frequently.

The entrance wound was clearly identifiable on the right temple, and Obie estimated it was two centimeters in size. The exit wound involved about one-fourth of the skull on the left, the broken bones palpable under the doctor's fingers. A puddle of dark burgundy blood covered the ground under the head, and globs of tan and grayish gelatinous brain remnants floated in the sanguine sea. Chunks of pale yellow bone fragments were scattered about.

Obie recorded the demographics from the driver's license data that Officer Johnson had pulled from the DMV. He scanned his only CME-1 form, making sure he had collected the required information for completing the second form, still at his office. Last, he retrieved the thermometer, noting the 78 degree reading.

"Let me call the Richmond office," he said. Retreating to his Jeep, he called the answering service on his mobile bag phone and let his vehicle run to warm up while he waited for the Richmond central district to return his call. Hardy depended on the cumbersome bag phone because service in his rural county was spotty and his roof magnet antenna afforded him better range. He waited for ten minutes, shivering and cold in just a jacket and no socks, trying to fill in the empty blanks on the CME-1 form. The idling Jeep seemed to share Dr. Hardy's shivering. Finally, the office called and accepted both the victims for autopsy, meaning Hardy did not have to collect toxicology and blood samples, a welcome break. The vehicle was now warm and, backing out of the driveway, he waved to Officer Duffer, who had emerged from the home.

He drove to his office to complete the second form on Mohammed Thacker and fax both to Richmond, making them available for the morning postmortem exams. At 4:40 a.m., he returned to bed to get an hour of sleepless rest before the workday began. When he arose the second time, his body was warmed again even if unrested. The first clothing he donned was a pair of socks.

Dr. Hardy attended his hospitalized patients at the local community hospital each morning. At age fifty, this daily task was a well-established routine, seven days a week. This morning was no exception, so he completed his rounds at the hospital and then headed for his office in Boydton, the Mecklenburg county seat. His wife, Lucy, was the nurse manager in his office, and she greeted him as he arrived. After fifteen years as a rural physician's wife, she was accustomed to having him called out during the night.

"Where did you go last night?"

"An ME case," he answered. He had left the original reports on the counter by the mail basket for her to mail. He knew that she would read over the reports and it would save him twenty questions to quench her curiosity. "Actually, two cases," he added.

"Oh," she said, picking up the CME-1 forms. She scanned the reports and said, without looking up, "Your first patient is in room 1."

Miss Gaskill, his first patient, had been Dr. Hardy's patient for fifteen years, following him to his present practice site. She had missed her last appointment, and some of her twelve prescriptions had lapsed. Now her blood sugar and blood pressure were out of control. Dr. Hardy was allowing his frustration to show.

"Well, I was meaning to make it last time," she explained, "but I was too sick to kick a chicken! I think it was the gas-i-litis or the demon-ticulitis."

Dr. Hardy smirked at the notion of being too sick to go to the doctor. He noted her weight—262 pounds. "Well, you're certainly not wasting away from it." As he handed her some updated prescriptions, he added, "You've got to take your medicines!"

"Okay, Doc," she said with a smile.

Later in the day, another hefty patient came in. Barney Wiles tipped the scales to 286 pounds. He was only five foot seven and lugged a massive gut when he walked. It was not strange that he always complained of knee pain, but he attributed this to crawling under houses as a plumber's assistant.

"I see, Mr. Wiles," said Hardy, "that you don't seem to have lost any weight yet."

"I don't know why, Doc. All I ate yesterdee was a half a sweet potato and some salad greens."

Dr. Hardy knew he was referring to turnip greens. "Well, that shouldn't be bad for your weight. What did you drink?"

"Only some water. Sodas swell up my siphonus," he stated, pointing to his midchest and throat.

The doctor knew he was lying. It would take 2,000 to 2,500 calories a day just to maintain his mass of living tissue. If he was eating as he described, he would be losing about three pounds a week. Dr. Hardy's office scales only read up to 350 pounds. His first set had a 300 pound capacity, but he had upgraded to the higher limit after a patient busted the spring lever on it. He currently had nine or ten patients who exceeded the new scale's limit.

"Here's a refill on your arthritis pain medicine. If you don't lose weight, your knees will wear out and need replacing. They're carrying two times the weight God designed them to carry."

"All right, I'll try," said Mr. Wiles. "But you know it's hard for me to exercise."

"Swim," suggested Dr. Hardy. The buoyancy of fat tissue in water would unload his joints. "We live near a lake with 800 miles of shoreline."

"I'll see," Mr. Wiles replied half-heartedly as he waddled down the hall.

Later that week, Clay Larrimore, the county sheriff, was in the office for his cholesterol check. He was tall and looked natural in the Western-style hats the county police wore. His manner was straightforward and matter-of-fact, and his age, late fifties, gave him a seasoned appearance.

"Did you get the autopsy reports on the Thackers yet?" he inquired.

"No," answered Dr. Hardy, "haven't seen them yet." He knew they might be in the mail piled up in his desk chair. "Did you?"

"Well, just the preliminaries. Appears drug-related."

Obie Hardy had returned to his hometown to practice, seeking a clean, rural environment to live in and raise a family. With his wife and their two daughters, he had laid roots in this community. People here were more likely to watch your back than to stab it. None-the-less, even in this small town of five hundred residents, there was no immunity to society's drug infestation.

Sure enough, when the autopsy reports returned six weeks later, they showed that Amanda had tested positive for cocaine and alcohol. The shooter, Mohammed, oddly enough, showed only alcohol, and below the legal limit. Life is the Earth's most valuable resource. It was a saddening waste to see young people's lives prematurely cut short.

The next medical examiner's call involved an obese person as well. The doctor stood in the home at 9:00 p.m. on a Thursday night, just out of town on the Skipwith Road. The house was a small, modular type building of only four rooms. Cynthia Montague, a black female weighing a massive 320 pounds at age forty-one, was lying supine, face up, on the bedroom floor. There was barely room to walk around her body, which competed for floor space in the small room with the bed, dresser, and chair. She wore gray sweatpants and a T-shirt, no shoes.

"She just had gallbladder surgery Monday," offered Buddy Moore, the EMT. "We found her like this when we arrived, dead."

Obie could feel the body heat radiating from her as he placed his Glad bag–covered thermometer in her armpit. Her joints were fully flexible—no signs of rigor mortis. Thick saliva was on her dusky lips, and her legs had an obvious amount of edema, or swelling. The axillary temperature reading was 93.4 degrees.

"Was she resuscitated?" asked Dr. Hardy.

"No, sir. She was gone by the time we arrived," stated Buddy Moore. Buddy was a tall black man in his early sixties. In addition to volunteering as an EMT, he did custodial work for some of the county offices as well as part-time duties at James Funeral Home. This residence was about three quarters of a mile from the rescue squad building, so the response time probably had not been long. People liked to know that everything possible was done for a dying family member. EMTs usually did the courteous, respectful CPR routine even when care seemed futile, to ease the family's burden of grief or guilt. Dr. Hardy wondered whether Buddy's affiliation with the funeral home could have affected his EMT judgment.

Dr. Hardy called the central district office to report the death and, as expected, was directed to sign it out as a "natural" death, a "green striped"—no need for an autopsy. Death certificates in Virginia were color-coded along the left border. A green-striped form designated a natural death, and a red-striped form signaled an ME case—suspicious, violent, or investigated. Dr. Hardy rarely used the yellow-striped certificate for fetal death. He surmised that a blood clot from her leg that had moved into the lung, a pulmonary embolus, was the likely cause and entered it on the death certificate. Since this was a natural death, Dr. Hardy would not receive any compensation for this scene visit. Hence, this case was a public service deed.

March brought Dr. Hardy's fourth ME case for the year, which represented some increase in frequency. At least this time he had been called at a reasonable hour and in the city of South Hill, where Dr. Hardy was finishing his hospital rounds on Saturday morning. The residence was on Dortch Lane in midtown. John Ramirez had been here from New Jersey, visiting his mother. She'd found him on the floor beside the bed at 9:30 a.m., and he hadn't been ill. Dr. Hardy found the body lying on the left side. He was a slender fifty-year-old black male and rigor [mortis] was complete, involving all extremities. He was wearing socks and slippers, making it seem unlikely that he'd died in bed. His temperature was 83 degrees axillary, giving an estimated time of death six hours earlier according to the chart in the *Medical Examiner's Handbook*. No bodily injuries were apparent, and all indications were that this death had been natural. However, since the death was unwitnessed and the deceased had been in apparent good health, the body would be sent to Richmond for postmortem exam.

The final autopsy report later verified advanced coronary atherosclerosis—heart attack—as the cause of death. It was refreshing to see a toxicology report showing no alcohol or other drugs. Although premature, John Ramirez's death had been a natural one.

Dr. Hardy noted that these recent deaths shared some similarities. Drugs or obesity had contributed to most of these premature deaths—unhealthy lifestyles. He wondered what role a family practice physician in rural Virginia could play in improving these statistics. He did make it a priority to attend the next local rescue squad training meeting and reviewed their practice protocols regarding resuscitation. There were only two times a basic EMT could not begin CPR: when a valid DNR—"do not resuscitate"—form was presented or when there were obvious signs of death such as rigor mortis, decomposition, or decapitation. Dr. Hardy noted that Buddy Moore was indeed present at the meeting and appeared to be attentive to the review. Hopefully, he would follow this standard in the future. Hardy decided he would also write an article for the local paper showing the county mortality figures and listing preventive health recommendations.

On Guard | 2

LAYMAR RICHARDS LOOKED FORWARD TO Saturday nights. He saw himself as a caterer, supplier of illegal refreshments for igniting parties. At twenty-six, he already was earning a generous income, despite barely finishing high school. He was five foot eleven, slim built, and a pencil-like mustache accented his dark skin. Claude, his point man, was stationed at the car wash in Chase City. Customers would call the phone booth and mention a code word, often Laymar Richards's nick name, Skeeter. They would then be given a location for pickups.

BRANG ... BRANG ... the pay phone sounded. Claude picked up the phone and waited silently.

"This is Jerry. I need Skeeter for a party bag."

"Warehouse on Fourth Street, 8:30." Claude hung up the phone and blended into the patrons of the convenience store beside the car wash.

Laymar Richards completed the exchange with "Jerry" in the shadows of the unlit Fourth Street. Unknown to Jerry, Claude was hidden around the corner of the warehouse. He held a twelve-gauge, double-barreled shotgun and was Laymar's insurance. Just before the appointment, Claude had scanned the perimeter and now remained vigilant while Laymar collected the three hundred dollars in cash. He couldn't hear the transaction but watched the steam puffs rise from their mouths in the cool, humid March air. Jerry drove off in a burgundy Ford Taurus.

Dr. Hardy was in the emergency room at the hospital in South Hill, having been called in to admit a patient with diabetic ketoacidosis. The police band radio broke its silence.

"Chase City Rescue 42 to South Hill ER. How do you copy?"

"This is South Hill ER. We copy you. Go ahead, Chase City," answered Patty, the head nurse.

"We're en route to your facility with a twenty-five to thirty-year-old black male in full arrest. He presented to the squad building by car unresponsive. Suspect drugs are involved. ETA [estimated time of arrival] six minutes."

"10-4, Chase City, we copy. Full arrest. Room Trauma-one on arrival."

Minutes later, the automatic doors swung open as the EMS team ushered in the stretcher carrying the subject. The ER doctor took over care, checking correct placement of the endotracheal tube. He directed the CPR to continue and tried IV epinephrine and cardiac shocks. After twenty minutes of this, Dr. Nguyen directed resuscitation to stop. Dr. Hardy was still in the ER, watching the outcome of the code blue. Dr. Nguyen walked toward him.

"You're an ME, aren't you, Hardy?"

"Yeah."

"This one's an ME case. Presented to the rescue squad building in full arrest. Some V-fib initially, but then only asystole. Young guy, probably an overdose."

Dr. Hardy began investigating the case. Reportedly, the man was named Shawn Terry and was twenty-six years old. A car had driven up to the rescue squad building in Chase City at 9:30 p.m., with the driver screaming for help. The deceased was lying in the floor board, unconscious, white powder on his nose and mouth. The female driver said he had been at a party.

"All we got was that the EMTs reported it was a Ford, probably a Taurus. Dark brown or burgundy colored," stated Deputy Wayne Harris. He was the investigating officer. He had short reddish brown hair and was about forty.

Dr. Hardy found no signs of violence. The pupils were dilated, probably from resuscitative drugs, and there was a persistent white, powdery residue on the upper lip. The body was still warm, 98 degrees, with no rigor mortis.

"Anybody come in with him?" asked Dr. Hardy.

"No," stated Nurse Patty, "but a lady called to check on him. That's how we got a name."

Dr. Hardy checked "pending" for the cause and manner of death on the CME-1 form, certain this was another drug-related county fatality.

Dale Gregory turned his white pickup onto Red Lawn Road, south of Boydton, and began looking for his meeting place. He slowed down as he neared the suspected dirt road entrance and hesitantly turned into it. He was thirty-eight with thick blonde hair and strong features. As a contractor, he often met customers at remote sites and was good at guessing locations. About one hundred fifty yards from the paved road, a pale green pickup truck was parked; it had rusting rear fenders and a mismatched tan colored driver's door. A Hispanic man who was leaning on the hood stood up straight. He wore a straw hat and had a prosthetic left arm. Dale was sure this was José Mortez, his intended appointment.

"Mr. Mortez?" Dale said, extending his hand. "I'm Dale Gregory."

José Mortez grinned, a golden incisor glistening. "Yes. Thank you for coming." He offered his right, real, flesh hand, as the prosthetic arm ended in mechanical steel pinchers.

"So … you need a barn built?"

"Yes. A special type of barn," he smiled. His Hispanic features and tanned skin obscured his age. He could be twenty five or forty five.

Mr. Mortez had an area laid out, with broken tree limbs staked into the ground marking the corners. It measured about forty by sixty feet, and he described a cement floor with a twenty-foot-wide circular pit near the center, with just a dirt bottom. To the side of the pit, he wanted four levels of concrete in a stairstep arrangement. His only elaboration was that the pit was for "manure" and the steps for "chicken roosts." The barn structure was to be a modular steel building.

"Well, I think I understand what you want. About twenty-four hundred square feet, cement slab, with some structured pourings. I'll get you a figure together in two or three days. I usually get about a 10 percent down payment when I start."

José pulled a wrinkled envelope out of his pocket and handed it to Dale. "Will this do?"

Dale thumbed through the stack of bills in the envelope, an assortment of hundreds, fifties, and twenties. "It looks like one thousand dollars," he reported.

"Sí."

"Let me get you a receipt."

"I don't need one," said José.

Dale was a bit wary about receiving small bills in a worn envelope, so he wrote out the receipt in his truck. This made the transaction seem a little less shady. "It helps me keep track," he explained.

"Okay."

"I can probably start in one to two weeks."

At his office, Dr. Hardy emerged from an exam room and recognized a familiar voice. A childhood friend, Josh Nichols, was in the back hallway laughing.

"Josh," he called out.

"Doc," replied Josh, peeking around the corner. "Sorry I couldn't stay in that exam room. I'm claustrophobic. They're no windows in there! I had to come out." He was about five foot six, muscular, a stocky 160 pounds. His hair was cut military style. Having lost his left leg to diabetes, he had hardly a limp on his prosthetic limb. "I just need some insulin needles and some pain pills for my stump—phantom limb pain." He retreated from the sunny back doorway to the windowless exam room. "It's good that you have dead bolts on your doors."

"Oh, yeah?" responded Dr. Hardy. "I suppose your work at the prison make you aware of security."

"Some, I reckon. But I'm a locksmith. I can pick locks, make keys, all that stuff."

"That's neat. I'll keep you in mind when I need new keys or locks."

"What I'm really best at is explosives, 'though. I've done some dynamiting for the Virginia Department of Highways."

"I guess that's handy for when you can't get a lock picked, too." Dr. Hardy knew Josh was a guard at the maximum-security prison one mile from town. But he hadn't known about Josh's experience in the Navy, working with underwater explosives, until his friend further enlightened him.

David Williamson was Dr. Hardy's next patient. He was a white man with a plethoric complexion, six foot four, and 296 pounds. His hulking size gave no hint of the kindness within him. This gentle giant had helped Dr. Hardy's practice by repairing cabinet hinges and loose floor tiles at his cost or less. He also worked at the local prison.

"I saw Josh Nichols in the waiting room," he grinned. "He's a legend at Mecklenburg Correctional."

"Like how?" asked Hardy.

"They have a videotape series for orientation of new guards. Josh appears in it repeatedly as examples of 'how not to do it.' He was stabbed in the thigh with a shank and shoved into a stairwell back when the Brileys were there. The monitor camera in the stairwell recorded it. He looked down at his thigh, jerked out the shank, and threw it down the stairs. Then, he grabbed the prisoner, threw him down the cement stairs, followed him to the landing, and kicked him senseless. Broke his wrist and a couple of ribs." David also recounted the summer that it had been intolerably hot in the non-air-conditioned guard towers. The polyester uniforms were so stifling that Josh had his prison insignia patches sewn into a white T-shirt. When he reported for duty, the warden prohibited him from working, citing the dress code, which specified a dress shirt, not just the patches. "Out front of the entrance, Josh went wild! He took off his T-shirt and started digging like a dog, throwing dirt back through his legs. He buried the shirt and drove off, bare-chested, in his beat-up black pickup. As he was leaving, he realized his patches were still on the shirt! He turned around, dug up the shirt, and drove off again! He got three days 'leave' for that stunt."

"Huh, I don't think I'd want to make him angry!" stated Dr. Hardy. "Anyway, here's the Diovan prescription for your blood pressure. And watch your weight!"

"Thanks, Doc."

Dr. Hardy was making his daily hospital rounds on a Thursday morning in June. When the "0" lit up on his pager, he called the switchboard.

"The sheriff's office needs a coroner," he was told. This case was at Mecklenburg Correctional Center, along the route to his office. He arrived at 8:35 a.m. and, after frisking, was escorted to the medical department.

The decedent lay on his back on the sole exam table in the department. His orange jumpsuit was open in the front, exposing his chest, where defibrillator pads were still in place. Chester Williams was a young black male, thirty-eight years old. His body was warm and still limp; he had been pronounced dead at 7:40 a.m. by the nurse, Shirley. This seemingly routine medical death struck Dr. Hardy as a bit mundane, given that he had prepared himself for a violent scenario, such as a stabbing or hanging. Dr. Hardy knew Shirley from when she had worked at the hospital. Her usual jovial nature was dampened by the gravity of this event as she recounted the man's medical history.

"He was in the ER four days ago with chest pain," she said. "Since then, he was taking Darvocet and ibuprofen for pain. He claimed to be dizzy and short of breath walking to pill call and breakfast. They rolled him in here by wheelchair with body aches all over and a BP of 70 over 60 at seven ten. Then he arrested, and we started CPR."

Dr. Hardy carefully felt the bones, especially the skull and neck, for any evidence of "unwitnessed" injuries. No bruising or puncture wounds were visible, except the IV in his right forearm. All Virginia prisoners who die while incarcerated were ME cases, usually requiring autopsies. This perplexing case was no exception. Williams was in on cocaine charges but had been locked up for two months. Since the body was accepted for autopsy by the central office in Richmond, Dr. Hardy was freed from collecting the blood and vitreous specimens. His paper report was all that was required.

The doctor was led back through the series of chain-link gates to the main entrance. The brief visit to a death scene here made him appreciate both life and freedom as he gazed at the intense blue spring sky spreading overhead. He couldn't resist looking along the shrubbery bed bordering the entrance, where he'd been told Josh Nichols had buried his shirt. Of course, there was no sign of a half-buried shirt, but visualizing the incident brought a smile to his face.

Once at the office, Dr. Hardy asked Lucy to fax the CME-1 form to Richmond while he began seeing his appointments. The ME case had caused a forty-minute backup in the schedule.

"Oh," said Lucy, "did you see your last final report?" She held out the yellow pages.

"No," he answered, taking the report. He scanned the documents. "Well, that one's no surprise," he commented, handing her back the report to file. Not unexpectedly, the final toxicology reports on Shawn Terry, the ER code blue fatality, confirmed the white powder to be cocaine, and cocaine toxicity (overdose), presumed accidental, was his official cause of death. The heart showed thickening of the left ventricle, usually resulting from high blood pressure, and some fibrosis, or scarring, typically seen in cases of virus infections, prior heart attacks, or drug-induced damage. Sometimes referred to as "holiday heart", these cardiac findings indicated chronic drug usage. There was also an additional finding of interest: two baggies of cocaine were present in his stomach.

At the Mecklenburg County sheriff's office, investigator Bruce Duffer read his copy of the autopsy report on Dr. Hardy's last ME case, Shawn Terry. It had to be signed out as accidental unless someone had suspicions that he had been forced to snort or given an extremely high concentration of cocaine. Upon questioning, all Shawn's associates had claimed they'd seen nothing, and hence, there was no evidence of plotting. Duffer completed his police report form, concluding "accident," but jotted a note to send to county undercover agents. A list of the people from the party could become persons of interest in their field work.

Spring Sailing | 3

THE THIRD SATURDAY IN APRIL was the first regatta of the season for the Clarksville Sailing Club. Obie Hardy had knocked down the wasp nest in the cabin of his vessel and inflated the trailer tires. Mike Crawford, who constituted his "crew," arrived at Hardy's house on time, just as he was gathering the sails, ice chest, and toolbox to load. Mike was six foot two, with coarse graying hair and mustache, and was on the stocky side. He was a former college athlete, but his fitness had waned a bit in his late forties. Yacht races still fanned that competitive spark enough to be exciting. Surprisingly, they arrived at Oconeechee Park for rigging and launch forty minutes before race time.

"Hardy," said Mike, as they tightened the stays for the twenty-five-foot mast, "you know there're no tags on this trailer."

"Yeah, but they're in the back of the Jeep."

"Those expired in 2004!"

"Well, we only drove eight miles. I don't think we'll have a problem. How about raising the keel up?"

"Aye-aye, Skipper," Mike responded as he started to turn the winch handle. "What's this in the handle, Hardy?" He pointed to a metal object holding the handle onto the winch axle bolt.

"Oh, that's a nail. I tried replacing the sheer pin, but it kept breaking. The nail has held up better."

"Hardy, sailing with you is always an adventure. Expired tags, arriving minutes before the race, bent nails holding parts together." Mike chuckled, climbing back into the cockpit.

Shortly, they were underway, Mike at the helm, pushing away from the dock. Obie pulled in the mainsail sheet to give the boat momentum as he lowered the keel. The wind was gusty as Obie set out the foresail to hoist. He left the racing genoa, the headsail, folded neatly below deck. The standard Dacron sails could endure the pounding wind bursts without altering the critical aerodynamic shape that the Kevlar racing counterpart must hold for maximum efficiency.

"We'll switch to the racing genoa at the starting line," he announced to Mike.

"Aye-aye, Hardy!"

"Okay, head 'er into the wind!" As they turned upwind, Obie raised the genoa smartly, the controlling sheet lines having been already threaded through the winch pulleys. It rustled loudly in the wind until he cleated the halyard line and called out, "Okay! Pull 'er in!"

The rustling quit as Mike Crawford pulled in the sheet line, and the sails filled taut with wind. The hull planed out as the boat gained speed. The vessel heeled up onto the right side as Mike sat on the upwind cockpit bench and toyed with the rudder control to balance the boat at about a twenty-degree list. *Second Wind* was now under full sail, setting a course for the starting line.

Twenty miles east of the regatta, another sailboat prepared to sail. Gary Layne was launching his O'Day 24, *Tipsy*, at Henderson Point. He was a faculty member at Vance Granville Community College and knew the North Carolina boat ramp well. It gave him easy access to the expanse of open water near the dam. At age sixty-six, he taught part-time and had a weekend cottage on Kerr Lake, as Carolinians called

Buggs Island Lake. He was tall, with brown hair graying above his ears. With *Tipsy*'s mast erected and auxiliary outboard motor running, he motored toward the big water. He handed the rudder handle to his partner in the cockpit.

"Keep it steady. Head straight out of the cove," he instructed Vicky, entrusting the steering to her. She seemed thrilled to be boating with her new boyfriend but a bit nervous at the helm.

"Okay," she smiled.

"When I hoist the mainsail, you'll need to steer us into the wind," Gary said, pointing out to the left.

"You'll tell me what to do, right, Gary?" she asked.

"Sure, mate," he answered, clipping the halyard line to the top of the sail, preparing to raise it. The protected cove had dampened the gusts of wind, and Gary was unprepared of their intensity. In his haste to impress his new mate and out of respect for the shallow water near the ramp, the keel had not yet been lowered—and sailboats were stable without a keel only when traveling downwind. He rapidly began raising the mainsail as *Tipsy* was clearing the wind shielding land point to the port side. "Turn into the wind, Vicky. Turn to the left," he called out.

Vicky pulled the tiller handle toward the left, not knowing that this was unlike steering a car and that she was supposed to pull in the opposite direction. As the mainsail reached the top of the mast, the boat turned right, across the direction of the wind, and was hit by a blast of wind.

"No! The other way!" yelled Gary. "Push the handle the other way!"

Vicky shoved the tiller to the right as the sail made a popping sound, filling suddenly with air. Without the pivotal keel, the boat jerked to the right and began rolling onto her side.

Back up the lake at Clarksville, the sailing club had finished its second race. *Second Wind*, not a high-performance yacht, had placed fourth in the field of six boats. Obie Hardy and Mike were sailing downwind toward the Oconeechee Park boat ramp. They left the racing genoa up since downwind sailing was calm and quiet, traveling with both the wind and wave forces.

"What's that noise?" asked Mike, hearing a soft clicking sound.

"Oh! It's my phone! It's in the ammo box," said Obie, referring to the watertight, steel army surplus case. He retrieved it from the cabin and snapped open the latch. It was his wife, Lucy.

"Where are you?" she asked.

"Cruising back to Oconeechee. It's been gusty but not too cold."

"I was worried sick! I heard a sailboat capsized on the police scanner. I've been calling you for thirty minutes."

"I'm sorry. I can't hear the phone unless it's quiet. We're on a run now. It's nice, now, but the wind has been tricky today."

"Well, be careful. I'll see you soon."

"Okay."

That week, the office blossomed with spring seasonal ailments—sinus inflammation, hay fever, and asthma. Latent joints emerged from winter hibernation and flared with arthritis and bursitis. Dr. Hardy wondered whether the mountain folks' "spring tonic" would ward off any of these maladies. An aspirin like substance is found in willow tree bark and the Mexican yam possesses a naturally occurring steroid. These might make effective tonic components.

"Here's the Aristocort," said Nurse Lucy, entering the exam room. "It's a hot commodity this week." Dr. Hardy had identified subacromial bursitis in the patient's shoulder and was preparing for an injection.

"Thanks." He took the vial of milky fluid and drew up a dose. "This isn't bad, Mrs. Carpenter. It's half lidocaine, which will numb you."

"How long will it work for?" she inquired, clearly a little concerned over the shot.

"If we're lucky, it will cure the inflammation, and it'll go away completely."

The following Sunday, the Hardy family had lunch after the church service in Clarksville. The two Hardy daughters, Vikki and Anna, disliked dressing up on weekends but tolerated the hour of church formality to eat at Subway. Afterward, they drove across the bridge heading home, with Buggs Island Lake expanding below them. The rich blue sky tinted the water's surface, wrinkled by waves that appeared motionless from the height of the bridge. *A perfect sailing day*, thought Obie. He startled, feeling a vibrating pulse in his left side.

"What is it, honey?" asked Lucy.

"Pager. I forgot it was on vibrate for the church service." He looked at the message and read it aloud. "9-1-1."

From his car phone, he called the unlisted non-emergency line to the 9-1-1 office. It was an ME case, on the lake. He shared this with his family.

"If you want, I'll go with you and fill out the forms. Would that help?" Lucy asked.

"Sure," he responded, knowing that her curiosity drove her offer as much as her generosity.

"I'll just need to change."

"Me, too," he said. "Never wear good clothes to an ME case."

They picked up the ME bag from the office on the way into town and dropped Vikki and Anna off at home to play with their neighbors. Dr. Hardy and Lucy changed clothes and set out on Route 707, which passed by their house. They drove out to North Bend Park, the popular camping area closest to the John H. Kerr dam. It was sparsely populated today because the season was still early; the water temperatures limited water sports to just fishing. The 9-1-1 operator directed them to the westernmost boat ramp.

They were greeted by a game warden who identified himself as John Hooper. He directed them to the V-hull boat he had beached there.

"It's a bit of a ride across there. Good thing you've got your jackets," he said. He was right. The sixty-degree sunny spring day became chilly as the boat speed created a twenty-mile-per-hour "breeze" that made Dr. Hardy's eyes water.

After about two and a half miles, they slowed as they approached a beach on the far shore. Dr. Hardy could see a bulge in the water at the shoreline, which he presumed was the body. An officer clad in county sheriff's brown assisted them ashore. "DIVE TEAM" was printed on the back of his jacket. Hardy recognized him.

"Aron," he said, "did you find him diving?"

"No, Hardy. Hooper found him scouting for fishermen."

"This is Lucy. She's a nurse," Hardy offered, validating her presence. She had already attached a CME-1 form to the clipboard and had a pen in hand. "Lucy, Aron Turner," he said. They exchanged greetings.

"This is presumed to be Gary Layne," Deputy Turner began. "His boat, a sailboat, overturned eight days ago. About a half mile down, toward the dam." Dr. Hardy thought it unusual that he had drifted upstream. "His girlfriend swam ashore. She said he started swimming at first, too, but went back to the boat and never came up."

Dr. Hardy pictured the ropes, or lines, floating in the water and sensed that he may have become entangled in them. Most likely, he had gone back to retrieve life jackets to assure his girlfriend reached shore in the chilly water.

"He was a professor at Vance Granville but had a lake cottage near Townsville. We haven't made a positive ID yet," Turner continued.

Dr. Hardy donned latex gloves and placed his thermometer in the water near the body.

Lucy started probing for data. "Do you have a date of birth or social?" she inquired. As she recorded the demographics, the doctor began examining the body. The deceased lay face down, with his head at the water's edge.

"Clothing: sweatshirt and shorts," he announced to Lucy. "Let's roll him over."

Hooper, in knee-high boots, and Turner, in waders, gloved up and rolled the man onto his back. The skin floated off the hands like gloves. Cool temperature retarded decay, but submersion in water accelerated the process. This was the end product—less odor and boggy, waterlogged tissues. The face was gray and swollen, eyes bulged closed. Hardy checked the skin under the sweatshirt for injuries, noting the trunk skin was also shedding. He feared evidence might float away if he did a more aggressive exam; the hand sheddings had now gone adrift.

"We need to get those skin pieces from the hands," directed Hardy. "They still may be fingerprinted."

"In these?" asked Turner, producing lunch-size paper bags.

"Yeah. Great." He recovered the thermometer. "Water temperature: 51 degrees."

"It's been warming about one to two degrees per week," observed game warden Hooper. "It was probably 49 degrees the day of the accident."

"He needs to go to Richmond for a post. We can't make a positive ID with this amount of bloating and decay."

When they returned to the boat ramp, it was nearly four o'clock. As they walked back to the Jeep, Lucy said, "That was the sailing accident I heard on the scanner when you were out sailing."

Deceit and Dealing | 4

DALE GREGORY FELT A GROWING uncertainty in his marriage. His wife, Sarina, had seemed more superficial lately, as if she were holding something from him. She had a careless way with credit cards and a frivolous lifestyle, traits that had excited him when they first met. Dale had decided to pocket the money from the cash job on Red Lawn Road and hide it from Sarina. He had opened a savings account in nearby Oxford, North Carolina, and for the address used a post office box he had rented in Bullock, just eleven miles over the state line. He listed his father jointly on the account. His father had helped his business in the past with equipment purchases and loans. The $7,200 balance had already yielded another $60 in interest. This would be a small shelter from the storm that was brewing.

His wife's car was gone when he pulled up to the house. He wondered where she might be until he found the note on the fridge. "Shopping in Danville. Will be home late. Spaghetti in the fridge. Sarina." He knew the spaghetti would be good because he had eaten it the night before. A beer and *Monday Night Football* would make the evening tolerable.

Sarina Gregory sat in her red Saturn in the Applebee's parking lot, carefully scanning the area to ensure there were no familiar vehicles around. She was a little early for her seven o'clock dinner date. Brad was usually punctual, but never early. The South Boston restaurant was far enough from Clarksville that the rendezvous might be secretive. Her pulse quickened when she saw Brad Wilkinson park in the side lot and walk briskly to the entrance. She saw him dart a glance at her car with a sly smile and continue to the door. As he entered, she opened her car door and followed behind him.

"You beat me here," he said when she entered, pulling her close to him for an embrace. He was just under six feet tall and straight, dark brown hair and a medium build. Sarina was an attractive thirty-five-year-old blonde, about five foot six. "Sarina, you're a breath of fresh air to me!" She smiled warmly, soaking up his affection. She felt his body's warmth through her blouse as they hugged.

"It's sooo good to see you too, Brad. You make me feel alive again!"

Their lust intensified throughout the cocktails and meal, driving them to an erotic pitch. A room at the Quality Inn provided accommodation for their after-dinner intimacy.

As they lay in bed in the warm radiance following orgasm, Brad was still inside Sarina as she said, "It would be so good if we could be together all the time." She lifted her pelvis forward, squeezing her groin muscles tight around him.

"Mmm," responded Brad, reflexively pushing himself back against her. "Yes, it would."

"Maybe, one day, we can stay together all night."

"That would be great," he said.

Detective Duffer assisted with the Mecklenburg County Drug Task Force, usually just referred to as "the task force." He was the local contact for an undercover agent assigned to the county by the Virginia State Police. Agent Randy Stephens had been in the community for six months with, unexpectedly, little to show for it. In the town of Chase City, he had identified Sandy Burton, a money handler for drug payments and debts. She would cash checks, written to herself, as payments for drug purchases or especially on accounts for "credit" extended to some customers. If questioned, buyers often explained these checks by saying she was a friend's girlfriend who needed medical care or an abortion or whose house had burned down. Sandy Burton would cash these checks, rotating banks, of course, and provide the dealer with cash or money orders. Officer Stephens, aka "Danny Hanes," had put together a list of buyers connected with Sandy, as well as the banks she frequented. His investigation had yet to produce evidence against the kingpin of drug trafficking in Mecklenburg County.

Stephens telephoned Duffer one Monday to report his recent reconnaissance findings. He had run across Sandy that Friday afternoon at one of her banks and followed her to two others, the last being First Citizens Bank in Chase City. From the Hardee's across the street, he had watched her eat pizza and socialize in the Italian restaurant. From there, she had made her way to the car wash at Purcy's Quik Stop. She parked her gray Cavalier in the middle bay and stepped out, wearing a tank top, shorts, and sandals. Sandy was a smallish girl, about five-three, early thirties with light brown, shoulder-length hair. Her hair color was probably why she was rarely addressed by her given name, Sandra. She wore sunglasses this evening, as the summer's daylight lingered, and nonprescription glasses at some banks. A few banks still knew her as Sandra.

Parked at the gasoline pump at Purcy's, "Danny" had watched Sandy. His height helped his vigil, and he had dressed inconspicuously in a T-shirt and blue jeans. He saw her gesture to a black male with a thin mustache who was walking from the pay phone at the parking lot corner toward the store.

"Excuse me, sir," she said, as if he were a stranger. "Do you have some change for the car wash?"

"I think so," he said, reaching into his pocket. He produced a handful of coins, mostly quarters. "Maybe five dollars."

She produced a wrap of bills from her pocket and handed them to him for the change.

"Five is good," she responded, releasing the five hundred dollars she had collected. She smiled and turned back toward her car. "Thank you."

"Sure. Maybe I'll see you around," said the man, heading back toward the pay phone that had begun to ring. BRANG ... BRANG. He lifted the receiver and listened silently.

Upon hearing this story, Duffer felt that Officer Stephens had developed a real lead. "Yeah. We can get a tap on that pay phone," he proposed. "This certainly looks suspicious."

"Okay. I'll keep my eyes open."

"Good job. Thanks."

That following week, the night sky was overcast with clouds, blotting Chase City with a deep darkness. Officer Stephens/Danny Hanes had wisely chosen this night to dust the phone booth at Purcy's Quik Stop for latent prints. At 4:00 a.m., the streets were quiet as he brushed the black chromatic powder over the receiver and cradle. He dabbed the clear adhesive over most of the surfaces since it was impossible to discern where the clearest prints might be. He also dusted the aluminum side shields and then cleaned off the surfaces with a damp rag before retreating with his prize. His goal was to collect physical evidence and confirm the identity of his suspected drug dealer. The wiretap would, hopefully, yield even more data.

Dr. Hardy was completing the admission orders on a patient with emphysema when the digits "9-1-1" lit up his pager. He called in and learned that someone in Baskerville had been found dead, and a medical examiner was needed. He didn't have his ME supplies with him, so he commandeered a CME-1 form, gloves, and a syringe from the ER stock. At least Baskerville was on his way back to Boydton.

Much of Mecklenburg County was off the beaten path, and this site was certainly no exception. He followed the 9-1-1 operator's directions and found himself on a dark dirt road. The dim glow of blue lights silhouetting the horizon assured Dr. Obie Hardy that he was not lost. As he stopped in front of a small farmhouse, a deputy walked up to greet him. It was 11:06 p.m.

"Dr. Hardy?" he said, "I'm Wilt Morris." Wilt was a clean-cut man in his late thirties with short black hair, and he stood about five nine.

"Yeah? I'm Dr. Hardy."

"He's by the van out front here," he said, gesturing. As they approached the vehicle, he continued. "This is Paul Green, forty-two-year-old white male. He was arrested on a DUI two days ago. Apparently, he drinks two half-gallons of gin a day. A friend drove him home about seven thirty, and he stayed out here in the van drinking."

Hardy noted someone on the ground beside the passenger door of the tan-colored van parked directly in front of the house. Wilt opened the van door, revealing a half-gallon gin bottle, about one-fourth filled with clear liquid. There were also three pill bottles in the floorboard. The body lay face up.

"He was checked about nine o'clock and was sleeping, still breathing. When he was checked on again at nine forty-five, he was unresponsive. His friend did chest compressions, but he did not respond."

Dr. Hardy noted there was no rigor mortis, indicating he was less than four hours dead. The pupils were small, three millimeters, a little unusual in deaths. He looked for the drug identities on the prescription bottles. The Bextra bottle appeared full, and it was only an arthritis medicine anyway. The empty bottle was propoxyphene, or Darvocet, a narcotic, probably the cause of the small pupils. The third bottle was also propoxyphene but appeared nearly full, filled only one day earlier.

Just then, a middle-aged male, unshaven, wearing flip-flops, a T-shirt, and jeans, approached from the house.

"This is his friend, who found him," said Wilt Morris.

"Hi. I'm Dr. Hardy, the medical examiner. Do you know why he needed these medicines?"

"Well … he said he had lung cancer two years ago. He had a lot of chest pains, I guess."

Dr. Hardy recorded the basic information of birth date, social security number, and so forth. He then went to his Jeep to phone in his report. There was no cell signal.

"I tried to call the Richmond office," he reported to Detective Morris upon returning.

"I know. There's no service here. I got a signal out at the corner of that field," he said, motioning.

"Okay. I need to be sure they'll accept him for autopsy. Otherwise, I'll need to collect blood."

Hardy drove back up the dirt road, thankful for the dry weather. He looked at the letterhead of the CME-1 form for the phone number. The form he had was from the Tidewater District in Norfolk. He was in the Central District, Richmond-based. He called the hospital ER to get the correct number from their rolodex. After ten minutes, the central office returned his call and accepted the case for a postmortem exam. He drove back to the house and notified Wilt Morris before leaving for home. Cause and manner of death would be listed as "pending" for now, but an overdose was suspected.

When Josh Nichols returned to Dr. Hardy's office for his diabetic follow-up, the doctor was astonished that he brought a chart of his blood sugar readings.

"Don't expect me to do this again, Hardy," he stated. "I just want you to see that I *do* control my sugar."

"I'm impressed. Your A-1-C [a marker of diabetic control] confirms this, too." Hardy compared the handwritten readings to the lab results in his chart. "Seven-point-two. Much improved!"

"Thanks, Obie." His tone became more serious. "You know, I thought I might be having to see the prison doc. The commonwealth attorney has ruined my life."

"What do you mean?"

"That bastard Paul Mathis took my kids! He got a restraining order for their mother. No physical contact with her or the kids. Supervised visitation once a month." His eyes were glaring. "*She* cheated on *me!*"

Hardy felt Josh's intensity, as a snake coiled to strike. He knew Josh could be violent if provoked, like a wild beast. Josh continued. "If you ever hear of something happening to Commonwealth Attorney Mathis …" He paused. "Well, never mind."

Dr. Hardy was sure the commonwealth attorney had information indicating Josh Nichols was potentially dangerous and impulsive. Any of his associates would admit this. These judicial restrictions, however, were only fueling his fire.

Summer Heat | 5

Sarina Gregory was planning a secret beach getaway with Brad. She needed a cover story and had chosen a week she knew her husband would be busy.

"Dale," she said one morning, "can we go to Virginia Beach for two nights for free?" She held up the time-share promotional mailer she had saved for such an opportunity.

"Er ... maybe," Dale responded, pouring his coffee. "When is it?"

"The only opening they had left this summer was midweek, August 14 and 15."

"That's a Wednesday and Thursday. I can't go in the middle of the week."

"Aw," she said, feigning disappointment, "can't you change your schedule some?"

"No. The cement trucks are booked. It would put me weeks behind for those two days."

"Oh." She pouted, appearing rejected. Then, after a brief pause, she exclaimed, "Oh! What if Elizabeth from Newport News joined me? We could shop, lie on the beach, maybe have a few drinks! How would that be?"

Dale hesitated before answering. This would give her a mini-vacation, and she wouldn't miss out on the beach because of his work obligations. He sipped his coffee. "Well, all right, I guess." Elizabeth was one of her college friends, a bit of a party girl, but probably harmless. "If she can go with you, it would give you both a beach break."

"Great!" she exclaimed, jumping up to hug him.

"But you'd better behave yourself!" he added.

"Yes sir, Daddy," she answered, giving him a peck on the cheek. "I'll call her today!"

The county investigator, Bruce Duffer, had planned a meeting with undercover agent "Danny" Stephens to exchange information and refine evidence. Agent Stephens had collected his notes, suspect names, photos, and fingerprint data. They met at the rest area off I-85 near Bracey. At 3:00 a.m. and with Duffer driving an unmarked car, there should be no local people to connect "Danny" with the police.

"So," began Stephens, "this Sandy Burton is the cashier for the operation." He sat across the dimly lit picnic table from Duffer. Even in the dark, his undercover beard was discernible, masking his features. At six feet, he seemed tall even when sitting. "These latents [fingerprints] are from the pay phone at Purcy's Quik Stop, hopefully from this dude they call 'Skeeter'."

"Good. The phone tap we placed there gave us an MO and we're monitoring the pickup sites, like the warehouse," said Duffer. "We've ID'd ten regular buyers."

"I hope the prints give a positive ID on Skeeter."

"I'll run them through IAFIS [Integrated Automated Fingerprint Identification System] and hope for a match. You've done some good work, here! Thanks a lot."

"If we can find his supplier, this could expand. Maybe a regional or national network," said Stephens.

"We have other state agents working at those levels, too."

"Great. Maybe in three to four months we'll be set to prosecute."

Duffer nodded. "Hopefully. We'll meet again in three to four weeks. I'll get this processed and sent to the commonwealth attorney." He picked up the yellow Dollar General shopping bag of information. "Again, good job. Hang in there. We're all behind you."

"Thanks," said Stephens, smiling and seeming grateful that his work was valued.

It was two thirty in the afternoon when Dr. Hardy received the sheriff's office call for a medical examiner. He quickly finished the two patients already in exam rooms while Lucy scanned the others waiting to see if any needed urgent treatment.

"Call any other scheduled patients. I can see them in the morning," he told Lucy. "If anyone needs checking today, I'll see them after four thirty if they want to come back or wait."

"Okay, I'll take care of it. Hurry back."

Dr. Obie Hardy grabbed his ME bag and aimed his Jeep toward Bracey. He hated running the air conditioning in his vehicle, but the August afternoon heat made him consider using it. His destination was on Red Lawn Road, near Route 1. The mobile home at the scene was marked by two Mecklenburg County police cruisers. Stepping out of his Jeep, Hardy noted an odor of dead animal decay tainting the hot, humid air. Detective Bruce Duffer met him at the front steps.

"Dr. Hardy, this man was last seen a week ago. He lives alone. The gas man was checking his tank and noticed a foul odor around the far end of the trailor. No one answered his knocking, so he called 9-1-1." Detective Duffer was a Caucasian man of medium build with black hair and was in his midforties. Dr. Hardy had known him distantly for several years and had seen him before as a patient. Today he was garbed in blue paper shoe covers and a surgical mask, which he had pulled up across his forehead to unmuffle his speech. "You want a mask and booties?" he offered.

"No, thanks." The doctor had endured the formaldehyde and tissue decay stench of cadavers for six months of gross anatomy. He was used to the odors of diseased bodies.

"The body is in the back bedroom, straight down the hall," said Duffer, motioning toward the home and pulling his mask back over his nose with his other gloved hand.

Hardy entered the living room, which was a good ten degrees hotter than the eighty-eight-degree outside temperature. The windows were cranked open, and a fan on the floor was blowing the stench from the hall toward the open front door. There was a runner of paper overlying the hall floor, wrinkled by footprints of investigators. In the bedroom a ceiling fan was running on high over the bed. Lying prone, on his stomach, was the decedent. The skin was dark, blackened, and separated at the wrists, elbows, and neck, with gelatinous ooze seeping onto the bedsheets.

Dr. Hardy decided that the body temperature reading would be useless and proceeded to try to collect vitreous from the eyes. The eye globes shield this fluid from decay, and if any tissue specimens might still yield some toxicological data, these would be the ones. As he reached for his syringe, he noted that the liquid pool of decay had oozed over the side of the bed, forming a puddle on the floor. He placed his ME bag out in the dry, paper-lined hallway. Gloved, sweating, and near gagging, he aimed his syringe toward the head.

The body's head was facing away from the edge of the bed. To reach the eyes, he would have to roll the body over or approach from the side against the wall. He decided to stand on the bed and try. The ceiling fan forced him to bend over, his feet straddling the body. His gloved hand guided the needle to the eye socket, but the globe of the eye was an empty sac, collapsing away from the needle poke. He suddenly realized the ridiculous futility of his examination and shifted his weight to dismount the bed. His shoes then stood in one-inch-deep, rotting body slime. He regretted declining the detective's offer of booties. His exit was hasty.

Outside, in the sultry air, Dr. Hardy gathered the information on the mobile home's presumed resident. The heady odor still tainted the air, over one hundred feet from the trailor. The body was not recognizable in its state of decomposition, and the funeral home hearse had arrived to transport it to Richmond for positive identification. Dr. Hardy climbed into his Jeep and, after a moment, noticed that the odor was growing in intensity. He looked down and discovered his slime-stained Topsiders. He quickly removed them and tied them up in a plastic bag. He drove home barefooted. The smell penetrated the bag still, and he left them outside the house, in the screen doorway, upon arriving home. He'd let them dry and breathe and then clean them thoroughly before he could wear them again.

Sarina Gregory sat with her friend Elizabeth inside the Waterside plaza in Norfolk. It was air conditioned in the mall overlooking the river, the summer sun sparkling on the waves. They were oblivious to the hot, humid afternoon air outside as they nibbled on snow cones.

"Oh, let me call Dale," Sarina quipped, punching buttons on her cell phone. "He'd love to hear from you!"

"Okay," responded Elizabeth.

"Hello, Dale? … Yeah. We're shopping now at Waterside … Yes, I'm glad I came, too … Elizabeth wants to say hi." She passed the phone to Elizabeth and smiled as Elizabeth chatted with Dale. Her cover was complete now.

After bidding farewell to her friend, Sarina drove back to Virginia Beach for her rendezvous with Brad. It was 6:00 p.m. when she reached their room; it was technically a condo but seemed more like a motel room with a kitchenette. Brad had already checked in and was in his swim trunks, holding a cold Bud Lite. She felt sticky after her drive from Norfolk and longed for a cool swim. Brad handed her a margarita wine cooler.

"Oh, thanks, babe! I'll be changed in a minute so we can swim." Shortly, she emerged from the bathroom in her black and white zebra-striped bikini. She was drinking the last of her green-tinted cooler.

"Oh, yeah!" exclaimed Brad. "You look great!" Her skin was lightly tanned, her medium-length blonde hair was at her shoulders, and her curves were enhanced by her swimsuit.

"Thanks," she said. She felt great too, a bit giddy from the alcohol. She picked up a beach towel and snapped it at Brad's bare legs. "What you got packed in those trunks?" she teased and then fled from the room.

Brad chased Sarina to the water's edge, splashing with her into the cool surf. They embraced in chest-deep water. She felt the melée of his warm skin pressed enticingly against her torso as chilled fingers of water moved between them. Sarina felt the growing firmness of what was in Brad's trunks.

Returning to the room, Brad announced, "I made dinner reservations at Rudee's." He dropped his swimsuit on the bathroom floor, exposing his partially erect manhood. Swimming with bikini-clad Sarina had aroused him.

"O-o-oh!" said Sarina, dropping her top onto the floor as well. "I think I'd like an appetizer now!" Topless and touching Brad's member, she led him to the bed. He eagerly followed her lead and sat on the edge of the bed. She kneeled between his thighs and began licking him.

"Ah!" he sighed, as she glided her warm tongue along his organ and then used her whole mouth.

"Mmm," she hummed. Then, pausing briefly, "You're salty from the sea! I'll be ready for another margarita." She resumed her oral action. Brad was fully rigid, tensing and writhing forward in response to her motion. Her breasts brushed lightly against his thighs and he reached out to caress them. Her desire heightened. Her groins longed for what her lips were having. "I've got to have you, now!"

Sarina squeezed out of her bikini bottoms and climbed onto Brad, guiding him into her. Their union quickly peaked, and they lay in tranquility on the bed afterward.

"Will I need an oyster appetizer tonight?" asked Brad, holding her nude body against his. "You know what they say."

"All you can get!" she teased, giving him a warm kiss.

At Dr. Hardy's medical office, Lucy Hardy was talking to Loren, the CNA.

"So, I get home with the groceries, walk to the kitchen door, and I notice a smell in the backyard. It was like something was dead! I figured the dog had dragged up a dead animal. Then, I opened the screen door and almost puked! The stench was unbelievable!"

"What?"

"Obie's shoes were in the doorway. He'd gotten dead man juice on them at the ME case!"

"Yuk! What'd you do?"

"He tried cleaning them with saddle soap, then bleach, but it didn't help much. I threw them away." She lowered her voice to a whisper. "But don't tell him. They were practically new!"

"What're you whispering about?" asked Dr. Hardy, walking up with a patient's chart. He received only smiles and silence in response. "Well, Loren," he said, handing her the chart, "I'll need a stress test scheduled on Mr. Evans."

"Sure," she answered. She sniffed him before turning away. He looked perplexed; Lucy laughed.

The following week, the county sheriff's office called Dr. Hardy's office. "They have a medical examiner's case in Clarksville," announced Loren. It was three thirty, Friday afternoon. "We only have two patients left to see."

"Okay, we'll do those quickly, and I can get out of here. Lucy?" Dr. Hardy said.

"Yes?" she answered.

"Get my ME bag ready and check the prescription call-ins."

"Sure."

Dr. Hardy arrived on the scene off Shiney Rock Road at four-fifteen. Three police cars sat in front of the single-story brick house. The afternoon air was still hot and humid. Detective Bruce Duffer was on his cell phone, walking toward Hardy from the backyard. Duffer had his usual business-like, methodical manner about him, badge clipped on his belt.

"Honey," he said into the phone, "you remember how I told you I'd be there unless one of three things happened? … Well, number two happened … You go on, and I'll meet you there when I'm done … Okay." He put the phone in his pocket and turned to Hardy. "The body's in the back," he said, reversing his direction to lead Dr. Hardy. "No one's seen him for two weeks. Lives alone, depressed, he's getting divorced. His kid was supposed to come visit today. There was no answer at the door, and they smelled something dead. The officers entered the house. It was unlocked. They traced the odor back here." He gestured to the parked car near the back of the house. "He never parks back here. It looks like he was hiding the vehicle."

Dr. Hardy had noted the smell when they rounded the corner of the house. The car was a gray sedan with a garden hose duct-taped to the exhaust and running up into the trunk, its lid cracked open.

"Do you have a name yet?" asked Hardy.

"Presumed to be Norman Quinton. Matches the registration and history. Thirty-four years old."

Dr. Hardy peered through the closed driver's window and saw a gray form behind the wheel. He wore a red T-shirt, and his head was leaning against the driver's door, a baseball cap lying beside the neck. The face was bloated beyond recognition and the nose shortened by decay. Maggots were teeming in the nose, eyes, and mouth. Those soft, moist tissues had given them a fertile growth environment. Adventurous larvae had crawled onto the scalp, door glass, and windshield, leaving clear trails through the condensation that fogged the glass. They randomly squirmed about, drawing life from the dead.

"The car is locked," continued Duffer. "We'll need to break in." The thought of opening this Pandora's box of rot, an incubator of decayed flesh, on a hot summer afternoon, knotted Obie's stomach. From his own car, Bruce Duffer produced a steel thumper, designed to break automobile glass. "We'll break the passenger window. That way we can get photos and not contaminate the body with glass fragments." Duffer was implementing an organized plan.

Duffer reached from his position off to the side of the door, and the second thump shattered the window, sending him scampering away from the vehicle as the wall of stench erupted from inside. The detective's eyes teared copiously as he struggled to photograph the scene.

Dr. Hardy kept his feet and shoes away from under the sides of the car. He wondered if Bruce was going to change clothes before meeting his wife at their social function. His odor would be disturbing, even at an outdoor event. The ME thermometer registered an air temperature of 96 degrees.

Photos completed, Dr. Hardy checked the condition of the body. The skin had sloughed off the fingertips, probably prohibiting fingerprint identification. Decay and bloat had made visual ID impossible. "He'll need to go to Richmond for ID and autopsy," he stated.

"I figured that," stated Duffer. His hands were gloved, so he used his shoulder to blot the sweat flowing down his face.

"I guess you'll change clothes before you go out."

"Oh, yeah. I'll shower, too … although my BO can't hold a candle to this!"

Dr. Hardy drove back to Boydton, his windows down for ventilation. He turned into Rudds Creek recreational park and parked at the swimming area. He changed into a pair of shorts that he kept in the back of his Jeep and waded out into the lake water. This cooled him off and rinsed away some of the fetid odor. He put his tainted clothing in a Wal-Mart bag and continued home.

"Where're your clothes?" asked Lucy as he entered the back kitchen door.

"Outside, in a bag. I had to rinse off at Rudds."

Her eyes widened as she glanced toward the backyard.

Obie knew she was a neat freak and feared another toxic contamination. "Relax! No dead man juice! It was just very hot and a lot of odor."

"Okay," she said, somewhat uncertainly. "But you'd better not ruin supper!"

He dared not admit that he didn't have much of an appetite just yet.

Sunday Fights | 6

THE COOLER OCTOBER BREEZE TICKLED the tree leaves, many with gold and orange tints already, sending them hurrying to the ground. Laymar "Skeeter" Richards drove up a sparsely graveled drive toward a white double-wide house about two hundred yards off the highway. A black pickup truck was parked near the house, lightly layered in fallen leaves. As he parked, a loud boom broke the silence. Startled, he quickly looked about to ensure he was not under gunfire. He grew a little uneasy when there was no response to three rounds of knocking at the door. As he returned to his car, he heard a rustling of leaves. A man was emerging from the back woods, dragging a large object. It was a fresh deer carcass, probably 110 pounds.

"Hello. I'm Laymar Richards. They call me Skeeter."

The man grinned back at Skeeter, releasing his hold on the deer.

"I'm looking for Mr. Josh Nichols," Skeeter continued.

"That's me. They call me Josh," the man answered, looking Skeeter over as if he was choosing a cut of meat at the butcher.

Skeeter nodded. "Is deer season in now?"

"Well, technically, it's only 'black powder' season, if you know what I mean," Josh said with a smile.

Skeeter noted Josh had no gun with him. He was certainly glad that his "white powder" was always in season. "Er … I might could use your services, if you're interested."

"All right. Come inside," he said, opening the door that was not locked.

"Word is you know about explosives," said Skeeter.

"Some," admitted Josh.

The living room was littered with shotgun casings, plastic jars of gunpowder, and various-sized metal pellets.

"Oh, these are just some shotgun reloads I'm doing," Josh said, noticing Skeeter's examination of the decor.

"I see." Skeeter nodded. "There's a certain collection of papers or files I would like to have burned, if you know what I mean." He studied Josh for his reaction.

"Destroying evidence, huh?"

"Yeah. Something like that."

"And where might these 'papers' be kept?" queried Josh.

"In the commonwealth attorney's office," stated Skeeter.

"Paul Mathis?" quipped Josh.

"Yeah."

"Well," Josh said with a grin, his eyes gleaming, "let's see what we can do."

Sundays were slow days for sales, Laymar noted as he waited at the warehouse on Fourth Street for a regular Sunday customer. José Mortez approached in his pale green pickup truck with the tan colored door.

"Amigo!" addressed Skeeter.

"Sí. Amigo," José responded, his gold tooth gleaming.

"Just where do you find to party on Sundays?" asked Skeeter. He was as much curious as he was seeking potential business opportunities.

"Well … I go to the derby."

"The derby? You race horses?"

"No, amigo," José said, looking about cautiously. He then whispered, "Cockfights."

"Cockfights? Around here?" queried Skeeter quietly.

"Sí," said José softly. "Red Lawn Road, near Baskerville. Four o'clock." He smiled and then said at normal volume, "Maybe you come some day."

"May be," he answered pensively as he pocketed José's money.

The following Sunday afternoon, Skeeter got another call from José. "How about I deliver it to the fight?" Skeeter offered.

"Very good. We'll see you there!"

Skeeter met José at the Sunday afternoon derby, making good on his delivery. As they walked about the chicken barn, a silver-toned Cadillac pulled into the parking area.

Cortez Trejo parked his Cadillac at the chicken barn on Red Lawn Road. Little Miguel, his son, was sleeping in his car seat in the back. It was Sunday night, six o'clock, a little early for his son's bedtime. Since the autumn evening air was still warm, Cortez partially lowered the rear windows. It was loud at the derby, so after turning off the engine, he cut the ignition switch back to the AC position so the radio could mask the clatter with soothing sounds. Maybe Miguel would sleep while he went to the fights.

Skeeter Richards was finishing his tour of the chicken barn, exiting with José. They met Cortez Trejo just outside the entrance, drinking from a pint bottle.

"Amigo," said José. "You know there's no drinking inside the barn?"

"Yes, yes," Cortez said, nodding. He turned up the bottle, swallowed the remaining contents, and dropped the empty into the trash barrel outside the door.

"Ten dollars," requested the door girl.

"Sure," answered Cortez, handing her the bill he had out already.

"Pretty tight ship," said Skeeter admiringly. "No drinking inside, cover charge, and concession sales. I like it."

"Yep. Can't be too careful, you know."

"Maybe I'll hang out here some days, if it's okay. Any activity can be improved with some 'seasoning.'"

"Sure. Sometimes the winners like to celebrate on the way home."

About twenty minutes after his father left, little Miguel stirred to consciousness and looked about the car. Being just eleven months old, he had only rudimentary ambulatory skills. He pulled up in the backseat and looked curiously at the cracked open window. As he stepped onto the door armrest, he inadvertently activated the electric window switch. The window glass lowered until, as he grabbed the top edge, his weight shifted off the control and the window stopped. Miguel leaned his head out of the window, changing his footing. The window began rising upward.

Cortez Trejo staggered slightly as he left the barn, returning to his car. The alcohol seasoning had warmed his extremities. There was an odd shape on the rear window of his car, as if someone had stuck something in the window crack. As he approached, the horrifying reality set in—it was his child's head wedged in the window!

"Ah-eee!" he screamed, rushing to open the door. "Help! Help! Ayuda!" He lowered the window and pulled his son's lifeless body from the vehicle. Little Miguel's head was dusky blue, although his body was still warm as life. "Mi Bambino, mi único, mi chico! Help!" With trembling, hands he laid the limp child on the ground. Not trained in resuscitation, Cortez was helpless but frantically attempted to do something–anything. He blew clumsily into Miguel's nose and mouth. Between sobbing, he repeated this action over and over. A solemn crowd was gathering.

Skeeter noted that José appeared petrified as he watched Cortez and his son. A death here, no matter how accidental, would expose his dynasty. The police would have a field day. José glanced nervously about, his panic obvious. Skeeter gently touched him on his real, right arm.

"Amigo," said Skeeter softly, "we can not help that poor man's boy."

José nodded, accepting that this was true.

"It would be devastating to the fights if the cops come out here." Some visitors were starting to scatter already. "Maybe I can help you with this delicate problem."

José looked up, his eyes pleading. "Yes. Yes!"

Dale Gregory was returning home from North Carolina. He had done the end-of-season maintenance on his family's vacation beach cottage near Morehead City. Sarina usually accompanied him on these excursions, but she had declined this time, having come down with a "bug" or something. It had still been a good weekend since he had caught some nice bluefish surf fishing and had collected three hundred dollars cash for some neighbors' handyman jobs. He added this to his secret savings account in Oxford on the way home. The account had grown over the past six months to more than eight thousand dollars.

At his driveway, he emptied the roadside mailbox. As he sorted the mail at the kitchen counter a few minutes later, the MasterCard bill caught his eye because the envelope was labeled "URGENT." Sarina usually took care of the household bills, but out of curiosity, he opened it. There had been no payments for two months, and the balance was $16,400! He stared incredulously at the statement for a minute. This was three months' income for him! He hated borrowing money and had built his home himself, over two years' time, paying as he went. He confronted Sarina with this when she came home.

"Oh, that. I was late making a payment, and … I bought some stuff at the beach. Don't worry, honey. I'll catch it up in the next month or two."

"You know they charge over 18 percent interest, don't you?"

"Well, I said I'll take care of it! I'll just take some money out of savings."

That didn't comfort Dale any. On Monday, he called MasterCard and found the current balance was $17,500. To assure himself, he also called on his Visa card and discovered another $12,400 due! Nearly $30,000! This was no minor thing! Sarina worked part-time at the cosmetic counter in Peebles. She couldn't pay off these bills in two years. He would cancel the cards to prevent further debt accumulation.

Dr. Hardy was making hospital rounds Tuesday morning when he was paged by the county sheriff's office. They needed a medical examiner in Buffalo Junction, the opposite end of the county. It would make him an hour and a half behind for office appointments, but he agreed to go. His civic duty called.

He was on the location by 9:05 a.m. It was a burned house with mostly cinders remaining, still smoldering.

"The fire was reported at 4:45 a.m.," reported Detective Duffer. "We weren't sure if anyone was home. A neighbor reported it."

"Anything look suspicious?" asked Hardy.

"I don't know yet. We haven't done a fire investigation yet. We found the body, or the remains, at about eight twenty."

Dr. Hardy looked at his shoes as he followed Duffer, stepping onto the bed of wet ashes. *This job is hard on footwear*, he thought.

"The resident was Michael Edwards, last seen at 10:00 p.m. We found these parts by the refrigerator."

There was a chunk of meat, twice the size of a ham and similarly shaped. Dr. Hardy identified it as the left side of the pelvis and thigh. Off to the side, Duffer showed him some bone fragments he had uncovered. These were half of the right femur bone and six vertebrae.

"There's possibly some usable DNA deep inside the hip for identification," stated Hardy. He placed the thermometer on the black ash bed for a scene temperature: 110 degrees.

"I'll sift through the ashes to look for more remains," said Duffer.

"I'll also collect some samples for chromatography, searching for accelerants." Duffer was an arson investigator for Mecklenburg County and enjoyed practicing this skill. His creed dictated that there were only four causes of fires: natural (lightning), accidental, arson, and undetermined. He hated the uncertainty in the "undetermined" label and looked intensively for evidence indicating any other cause. Starting a fire investigation seemed to light him up.

"All right. I'll fax what we've found to the central office," said Hardy. He examined the body diagram on the CME-1 form; it didn't lend itself well to demonstrating a few skeletal-like body parts. The doctor did his best to sketch in his findings and then headed back to his office

At the end of the office day, Dr. Hardy stayed alone, sifting through his pile of mail. The autopsy report on the car suicide case, Norman Quinton, was back. The identity had been confirmed through comparison with premortem X-rays. Extensive decomposition set time the death as four to five days before, presumed from carbon monoxide poisoning. These recent ME deaths, all people his age or younger, were placing a heavy burden on Dr. Hardy's shoulders. Death, by the grace of God, had spared him for now.

At home, he sought haven from this load. Lucy entered the kitchen as he walked through the door. "The preacher said Mickey scared and chased some kids playing in the lot behind the church today," she reported. Mickey was their dog.

"Oh? Was anyone hurt?" responded Obie.

"No. Just scared."

"Were they the same kids that were calling Mickey last week and then throwing sticks and rocks at him?"

"I think so."

Obie Hardy didn't want to belittle this neighborhood crisis, but in light of the tragedies he had dealt with during the day, it seemed awfully trifling.

"Maybe we can tie him during the day. It's hardly fair, though, since they were teasing him first. Mickey's a good watch dog, and we're away from the house a lot."

That night, at bedtime, Obie massaged Lucy's back. Sometimes this would lead to more intimate activity, but not this time. Recently reminded of his own mortality, he was appreciating life by feeling the touch of live, clean, soft flesh with his hands. It felt good to feel her warm body lying in bed with him.

Schemes | 7

"THIS IS THE 9-1-1 OPERATOR. Is this Dr. Hardy?"

"Yeah."

"We need a coroner at Eastland Creek." It was 9:55 on a Monday night.

"Okay. I'll be there in about fifteen minutes," Dr. Hardy stated. At least it wasn't in the wee hours and the scene was only four miles away. The October night was not harsh, still mild with no precipitation or wind. Since Eastland Creek had no overnight camping, this had to be a drowning, probably a bass fisherman. The telltale red and blue flashing lights summoned him from the graveled park entrance road. The lights weren't by the boat ramp, however, but rather were up beside the picnic area. An inquisitive Dr. Hardy approached the assembly. "I thought for sure this would be a floater."

"Well, technically, it is," said Bruce Duffer, who was once again the on-scene investigator. Dr. Hardy scanned the surrounding area. No body was visible. The only structure nearby was the outhouse-type toilet.

"They're not on the john, are they?" asked Hardy.

"No," answered Duffer, as a deputy passed to him a long aluminum pole with a hook on the end. "They're *in* the john!" They walked over to the outhouse, and Duffer shined a flashlight down the toilet pit. Hardy saw a fleshy mound bobbing above the surface of the sewage.

"My God!" exclaimed Hardy. "They must call you for the *worst* cases!"

Two deputies lifted the commode off the cement floor of the outhouse and placed it outside on the ground. They prodded the small body with boat hook poles, but it only bobbed away.

"Let's try the net," suggested Detective Duffer, removing a large fish net from his trunk. With teamwork, flashlights, a hook, and a net, they lifted the body from the foul liquid onto a white sheet spread out on the ground. Dr. Hardy began his exam.

The skin was thickened and leather-like on the child's torso. The color was manila. Dr. Hardy thought the child might be Caucasian, the skin stained from feces, or light skinned black, with the skin bleached by the sewage chemicals. Or, most likely, the deceased was Hispanic or Asian. The septic enzymes had eaten away the fingers and toes; bone and tendon stumps protruded from the hands and feet. The body lay supine, and the skin of the crotch was eroded, with no genital structures remaining. Hardy was taken aback. This was his first sexless corpse. No fingers for prints, no definite race, not even a sex. What could he do to help with this case? *Growth charts*, he thought.

"Anyone have a measuring tape?" he asked.

"I've got a yardstick," reported Duffer, producing another useful item from the trunk of his Ford Crown Victoria. It wasn't as high-tech as the Batmobile, but it was this rural county's crime fighting unit. Dr. Hardy placed it alongside the body and estimated a length, or height.

"Twenty-seven and a half inches." He could use his pediatric growth charts to approximate an age. A head circumference would help, too. The head was a leathery sack; its contents had been dissolved by the chemicals and decay. He posed the head sack into a rounded shape and wrapped a string around its perimeter. The head collapsed flat when he released it. He stretched the string alongside the yardstick.

"Seventeen and three-quarters inches," Dr. Hardy announced, although this number was meaningless to the onlookers.

The Eastland Creek landing was a day-use area and not staffed by park attendants. There was an honor-system pay box to leave launch fees and vehicle information to avoid being ticketed by patrolling rangers.

"I'll pull out the vehicle registrations," offered the Corps of Engineers ranger. Dr. Hardy was sure the body dropper hadn't registered his vehicle. "Maybe someone saw something suspicious."

"Okay. And do you know when the last sewage treatment was done here?" asked Detective Duffer.

"I'll check. They usually come once a week."

"Good. Dr. Hardy?" asked Duffer. "Could this body have been here over a week?"

"I don't know how fast the chemicals would digest the body, but from the looks of this, easily a week."

Obie Hardy drove down to his office before returning home. He was too disturbed by this case to go right to bed. He pulled out a pediatric growth chart, selecting the male form. Since there was such complete decimation of the genital tissue, he felt that the protrusive male organ could have been bathed in the caustic chemicals. The folded female genitalia would have been somewhat more protected from decay. According to the fiftieth percentile, the victim would have been ten to twelve months old. This CME-1 form was very incomplete—name, "unidentified child"; sex, "unknown"; age, "estimated 10 to 12 months." Maybe some acceptable DNA tissue could be salvaged. He hoped that this was simply a natural or accidental death in a family that could not afford funeral expenses. Any other scenario would be more heinous. He faxed his report to the central office and turned out the lights.

Skeeter sat in Josh Nichols's living room/hobby area as Josh presented his handiwork. Josh was as proud of his creation as a new daddy. It was a dual system with a small powder charge for detonation and dispersal of about a quart of homemade napalm. A foil pouch held the volatile napalm gel mixture.

"I rigged a simple clock delay timer for the trigger," explained Josh. "We could use a remote device, like a cell phone or pager, but it'll cost you extra."

"That's okay," answered Skeeter, feeling quite pleased with the product. "I can just set it for later, at night, maybe a twelve-hour delay."

"No problem. But the napalm is just a fire bomb, spreading the fire through about a room-size area. Sort of gasoline in a gel. There won't be significant blast damage."

"Perfect! Now, what should I put it in? A briefcase?"

"Well … maybe a nylon or vinyl case to allow maximal dispersal."

Skeeter nodded his understanding. He was excited to see his plan materializing.

"Now, about the fee …" continued Josh.

"Yes. Fifteen hundred was what we said." Skeeter laid an envelope in front of Josh. "Seven fifty now and seven fifty after successful detonation."

"That's fine."

"Now, can I use your bathroom?" he added.

"Sure. Across the hall," answered Josh, beginning to count the bills.

Skeeter noticed, on the shelf beside the sink, insulin bottles, syringes, and alcohol pads. The trash can under the sink had blood-stained cotton balls, alcohol packages, and two empty insulin vials. He had an idea. While the toilet was flushing, he retrieved an insulin bottle from the trash.

Sarina and Brad were enjoying the seafood buffet at Ernie's Restaurant in South Boston.

"Not bad," commented Brad, "but it's not Rudee's at Virginia Beach. He smiled at Sarina.

"Yeah," she answered half-heartedly.

"What's wrong, honey?"

"Dale has found the credit card bills and is harassing me about them. I don't know how much more I can take!"

Brad paused, adopting a serious air. "Well, have you thought about divorce?"

"I don't think I'd get much. All we've got is the house and his business equipment. I don't want a house in Buffalo Junction if I get divorced!"

"Does he have any other property?"

"No. Just his life insurance."

"Well, I doubt he'll accommodate you by just dying."

"I don't know…" She paused, her expression pensive. "Probably not … at least not by *natural* causes." She peered up at Brad sinisterly, with her brow lowered.

Brad couldn't tell whether she was scheming or joking. "I still think a divorce might be simpler," he responded.

"Yeah, I guess so," said Sarina, pouting. "But $250,000 in insurance money still sounds good. And if he died *accidentally*, it might pay double!"

Brad was an insurance agent and would know that this was a standard feature of most life insurance policies. She was definitely having serious thoughts.

Just then, the waitress interrupted. "Can I refill your tea?"

"Sure! Thanks!" answered Brad, eagerly redirecting the conversation. Was his love for Sarina and desire for their clandestine relationship to be legitimized worth the price of a felony crime? "I think I'll get a few more hushpuppies," he continued. "You want anything?"

"Nah. Thanks," she said, smiling weakly.

Friday night, Obie and Lucy Hardy ate supper at Rose's, the local pizza place. Their daughters were off with the high school band to an away football game. They were walking the two blocks home when the 9-1-1 office called. They sometimes just called Dr. Hardy's cell phone instead of going through the paging beeper. He had finally exchanged his bag phone for the pocket sized one, but only when his battery had died and had been phased out of production.

"We need an ME at a highway fatality," reported the dispatcher.

After getting the details, Obie hung up and Lucy asked, "An ME case?"

"Yeah. Car wreck," he answered.

"I'll ride with you if you like."

"Sure." He would appreciate a helping hand as well as the company. This would require blood and vitreous samples if an autopsy was not needed. "It's in Bracey."

The scene was on Nellie Jones Road. The flashing golden lights of the tow truck accented the pulsating red ambulance lights, giving an inappropriate festive air. The county officer in charge was Wilt Morris. He was clean-cut and wearing a neat white dress uniform shirt. He led Dr. Hardy to the ditch where a sheet hid the corpse.

"Apparently, an unrestrained driver lost control and was ejected from the vehicle," explained Detective Morris. "The resident here heard the crash and took the child inside."

"The child?" asked Hardy.

"Yep. Four-year-old daughter. She was ambulating with only minor injury. There appears to be alcohol involved."

Obie Hardy looked at Lucy, who had heard the details. They both felt relief that the child was unharmed but felt little sympathy for the irresponsible driver.

Dr. Hardy examined the body, a twenty-eight-year-old black male who smelled heavily of alcohol. The flanks showed some abrasions, but the fatal injury was to the head. A large scalp laceration was on the back of the head, and bloody vomitus splattered the nose and mouth. He may have choked on these fluids or had intracranial bleeding compressing the brain; either would be a consequence of the head injury. He deemed this the cause of death, accidental the manner of death.

After reviewing the case with the central office, Obie and Lucy started the drive home. "Can you believe someone would drive drunk with their daughter on board?" asked Lucy.

"No," Obie answered. "At least she was okay. The last kid I did was dumped in a toilet. People can be so uncouth!"

Bruce Duffer had a Monday appointment in Dr. Hardy's office for a routine blood pressure check. Dr. Hardy took a second pressure reading.

"Your blood pressure is better after sitting a few minutes," Hardy noted. "The first reading was elevated, though."

"I know. It's up and down with this job. A lot of stress." There were only four detectives in the county department. Duffer was the highest-trained and the best.

"Okay, we'll keep the same treatment regimen for now," said Dr. Hardy. "Oh, I saw the central office had enough DNA to ID the remains from that house fire. Did you determine the cause of the fire?"

"Well, we found no accelerants. He had a gas stove, and the fire originated in the kitchen. Appears it was a gas line malfunction—an accident."

"It's good that it wasn't arson. Any more info on the kid from the outhouse at Eastland Creek?"

"No. As you said, possible Hispanic or Asian race, maybe eight to ten months age. Still no clues as to who or how."

"It's sickening to me. I hope it was a natural death, and the parents simply couldn't afford a funeral."

"Maybe. Let's hope so."

Fire Strike | 8

DETECTIVE DUFFER HAD BROUGHT THE evidence file on "Skeeter" to Paul Mathis, the commonwealth attorney for Mecklenburg County, and left it for Mathis to review. Mathis was going to decide whether task force undercover agents had compiled sufficient evidence to pursue prosecution. His office was across the street from the courthouse in the Goode Building, a white-painted brick structure built on a sloping lot. It had single-story street frontage with a full basement and a two-story rear. Originally built as a bank in 1908, the historic building was a proud display of neoclassical design, with high-arched, tall windows.

As was typical of lawyers, he wore a dress shirt and tie while sitting at his desk. He was a tall man of modest build with white hair already at age forty-six. He looked up at the wall clock—9:50 a.m. He was due in court in ten minutes. A breaking and entering case was up, not very thrilling but part of the grind. He sighed and stood up. Donning his navy suit jacket and retrieving his briefcase, Mathis strode across the street and entered the court building.

Outside the court building, Sandy Burton was sitting on the cement retaining wall along the sidewalk. She watched Mathis make his entrance and then, as if on cue, stood up. Carrying a small knapsack as if it was an oversized purse, she walked leisurely over to the Goode Building.

The basement level housed county offices, such as the building inspector and zoning departments, as well as the commonwealth attorney's office. It also provided the operations office for the Mecklenburg County Drug Task Force. Sandy walked through the back entrance and found Paul Mathis's office. A secretary sat at the front desk.

"Can I help you?" asked the secretary.

"Yeah. I've got the itemized list Mr. Mathis needed for the Garner robbery—the values of the stolen stuff." Sandy held out a manila folder.

"The Garner case?" she said, grabbing the folder. "He's in court on it now. Let me run these over, right away!"

Sandy backed out into the hall as the secretary stepped briskly past her and out the back door. She then eased back in, passed the secretary's desk, and entered through the open door of Paul Mathis' office. She placed the knapsack on the floor beside his desk, behind the waste basket. Then, with a nonchalant air, she walked out of the building and turned down the street.

At Dr. Hardy's office, Lucy was phoning a patient with her test results. The Pap smear for Ms. Winston, a pleasant, middle-aged black woman, had revealed a sexually transmitted disease.

"Ms. Winston, this is Dr. Hardy's nurse, Lucy."

"Uh-huh."

"Your Pap test showed no signs of cancer, but it did show that you have an infection. A trichomonas infection."

"It does?"

"Yes. I can call you in an antibiotic, but this is sexually transmitted. We need to treat your partner, too."

"Well, I treats him good," reported Ms. Winston. Lucy held her hand over her mouth to muffle her laughter.

"I'm sure you do. But he needs his doctor to prescribe him an antibiotic, too."

"But he don't like doctors."

"Well, he needs treatment, too."

"Okay. But I treats him fine," she insisted. Lucy was still smiling when Dr. Hardy emerged from an exam room.

"What's up?" he asked.

"Some of *your* patients!" she answered.

"Someone from 9-1-1 is on the phone," interrupted Loren, leaning into the pass-through window from the front office.

Dr. Hardy took the call. A medical examiner was needed at the scene of a death. At least this call hadn't come in the middle of the patient schedule again, since, at 3:20 p.m., only four more appointments remained. Hanging up, Dr. Hardy addressed his staff.

"Okay, there's an ME case." He pointed at the schedule on the pass-through counter top. "I'll see Ms. Fields, and Lucy, you can check Mr. Thomas and refill any of his blood pressure medicines. And Loren, do a strept test on the sore throat case. Call me if it's positive."

"I'll call Ms. Martin, the four thirty, and try to reschedule her tomorrow," offered Loren.

"Great," said Dr. Hardy.

After the office shuffle, Dr. Hardy headed to the ME scene on highway 1, near the North Carolina border. The driveway was hard to find, since the police cruiser on the scene was fifty yards from the highway. Hardy passed by the turn but doubled back after reaching the state line. The residence was a small and ordinary white frame house, and Wilt Morris met Dr. Hardy there. Hardy had last worked with Morris on the highway fatality near Bracey.

"Dr. Hardy," Detective Morris began. "The decedent is in the back, near the woods. No one's seen him for three or four weeks. Last week, neighbors noted black smoke rising from behind the house."

Morris led Dr. Hardy behind the house, about fifty yards from the back side. The back lot was wooded, and there was a blackened area near the edge. The body was that of an elderly white male. He was lying on his side, alongside a pile of ashes from burned car tires, where the tires' steel belt ghosts still lingered. He was dressed only in a shirt and pants but was wearing a holster. The pistol, a thirty-eight caliber, lay between the body and the ashes. The muscles of the right thigh and calf exhibited some open wounds.

"There appears to be some animal damage to the right leg," noted the detective. Since the body was bordering the woods, Hardy wondered why there wasn't more extensive marring. The predator probably didn't like the flavor of human flesh, being unaccustomed to this prey.

"I'm surprised the animals didn't eat more," said Dr. Hardy. "I wonder if the fire had cooked him some."

"Apparently, he tried to burn himself. He lit the tires on fire, got up close, and shot himself in the head. Instead of falling into the fire, he fell to his right side."

On examination, the body was stiff with complete rigor mortis. A bullet exit wound was obvious in the back of the skull. Dr. Hardy could feel the broken bone fragments around the area. Rolling him over revealed an entrance site in his mouth.

"Who is he?" asked Hardy.

"The neighbor ID'd him. Calvin Bennett, ninety years old. He sees a doctor in North Carolina. We found a prescription bottle and a note in the kitchen."

Dr. Hardy knew that the elderly often have trouble dealing with loss of independence, especially the loners. At his age, this man would have been at risk for health problems and dementia. "Did he live alone?" he asked, as they walked back up to the house.

"Yeah. Unmarried."

They entered the house, and Dr. Hardy noted it was cold. "Is the heat off?"

"No furnace or heat pump. Only a fireplace and a wood stove."

The house was dim and gloomy, lightly soot-stained from burning wood. It felt depressing and inhospitable, as if a lingering cold cloud of despair permeated the air. The empty prescription bottle was for an antibiotic, prescribed by Dr. Lennick from Norlina, a nearby North Carolina town.

"We found this note," said the detective. "It says he wants his body cremated. I guess he just missed falling into the fire."

"Self-cremation. You don't see that too often."

The usual six weeks passed before Dr. Hardy received the postmortem results on Mr. Bennett. The autopsy had revealed that he had prostate cancer. His doctor had reported that the antibiotic had been for a urinary infection, and he had advised his patient to see an urologist. Mr. Bennett most likely had some urinary incontinence with the infection and felt he was becoming unable to care for himself. He probably assumed he had cancer and was dying and so decided to end life on his own terms. He had kept his ailments and worries secret and sought a lonely, harsh death, witnessed only by a few wild carnivores who nibbled at his carcass.

A week later, the fire siren awakened Obie and Lucy Hardy at 3:30 a.m. The loud whines cycled repeatedly, accompanied by Mickey's howling, before falling silent. Obie returned to a light sleep before arising at 5:45 a.m. for morning hospital rounds. He was oblivious to the intense inferno that had raged during the night, just two blocks away. He did notice a burnt odor in the air while walking to his Jeep but took no exceptional notice, since many rural homes were heated with wood. There was a smoke fog still rising from the building's ashes on Washington Street, one block over, blinded from his view by the courthouse as he drove past in the predawn darkness.

Detective Bruce Duffer stood in the charred, rubble-filled shell of the old Goode Building, the outer brick wall still standing. The white painted exterior was scathed with smoke trails. As a volunteer fireman, he had been busy for the past three hours suppressing the fire. The prolonged stress of the ordeal and the lack of sleep had left him fatigued, physically and emotionally drained. He was saddened by the loss of this historic structure, as much as if he had lost a friend. The damp morning air was thick with the stale, burnt smell, like that of a trash can fire. The volunteer firemen who had arrived first reported that the blaze seemed to have originated in the basement level of the northeast corner, by Jefferson Street. Duffer was certain the century-old structure harbored electrical wiring that likely was faulty. Assuming his investigator role now, he studied the fire patterns on the interior walls. The charring lacked the fan-shaped pattern often seen from a single-point source of origin and had more of a scattered appearance. This was not the appearance of a blatant electrical fire, which raised his suspicion of arson. He scooped up some cinders and sealed them in an unused paint can, another essential item that he had retrieved from his car trunk.

"Do we know what office was in this area?" he asked.

"This was probably either the zoning office or the commonwealth attorney's office," answered the plump Detective Johnson.

"Well, this seems a little suspicious," noted Duffer. He realized that the commonwealth attorney's office might represent a target, as might the Task Force office, which was also in the basement. "We'll need to interview the office workers while we wait for forensics to check for accelerants."

After finishing at the fire scene, Duffer groggily stopped by his office to check in, planning to drive home and shower before beginning his regular workday. His vision seemed blurred from the smoke, the heat, and exhaustion. Wilt Morris was at his own desk, adjacent to Duffer's, and looked up.

"How's the case going, Sherlock?" quipped Morris, smirking. Bruce Duffer was wearing his glasses, but the right lens was missing, giving him the appearance of wearing a monocle.

"Huh?" responded Duffer.

"Your glasses." Morris tapped his own eyebrow. "All you need is the sheriff's pipe to complete the look!"

Detective Duffer removed his damaged eyeglasses and realized that sometime, in the heat of battle, he had lost a lens and had been too involved in the ordeal to even notice.

"The spoils of war, Sir Watson," he said.

Skeeter Richards knocked on the door of Josh Nichols's house.

"Yeah. It's open," Josh called out.

Skeeter opened the door and entered, smiling. Josh was sitting in his living room reading the county paper, *The News Progress*. The front-page photo was of a burned building in Boydton, the Goode Building. Josh reached for his prosthetic leg, which was leaning against the couch.

"Mr. Nichols, I had my doubts about you, but you've impressed me," began Skeeter. "Your work exceeded my expectations!"

"Yeah, well, explosives are my specialty. I was reading about a local fire," he said, pointing to the local headline. "They seem to think it may be arson."

Skeeter smiled, contented. "I've brought you the balance of your fee. Thanks for your work." He handed Josh an envelope of money.

Josh accepted that the amount was adequate without checking, having counted the first payment. It seemed his satisfaction that Paul Mathis had been dealt such a blow was payment enough to him anyway. He pocketed the envelope and grinned. "Anytime."

"I hope it won't be necessary again. Oh, can I use your bathroom again?"

"Yeah. Sure."

Skeeter walked into the bathroom and again found the insulin supplies on the shelf. After a quick glance over his shoulder, he picked up and pocketed the bottle of clear insulin. To avert any suspicions, he urinated in the toilet, producing the expected pouring sound. He replaced the insulin vial with the one he had taken before, now reformulated.

As he returned to the living room, he turned to Josh. "Well, this concludes our venture. Oh, and if anyone asks, we've never met."

"Sure thing, stranger. Advertising is not my style, if you know what I mean."

"Yes, I think I do. Good-bye, Mr. Nichols."

"Same to you."

The Spoils | 9

RAMOS ANGELIS WAS A REGULAR at the Sunday fights. Cockfighting was a weekend tradition in Mexico, and the derby engendered a nostalgic comfort for Ramos. He was seventeen when he entered the States two years ago and had grown to a slender five-eleven now. His wages were usually paid in cash, since his domicile here was not legal. He had $150 in his pocket and two tequilas in his gut when he entered the barn.

José Mortez was at the pit, checking the sizes of the metal gaffs, or spurs, to assure fair competition. He enforced the US standard of two inches. Although there was no rule as to which leg a gaff was attached to, most cockers preferred the left leg.

Beside the pit stood Johnny Bohannon, a breeder from eastern Virginia, who had brought three cocks to this week's derby. He raised roundheads, a fighting strain developed in Massachusetts in the 1860s. The original stock had been imported into Boston from England, and the signature feature of small, rounded heads gave rise to the name. Roundheads were an intelligent breed renowned as superior fighters.

Chavis, a Mexican farmhand, was in town for the derby too. He usually worked the fields in Tidewater but knew some of the locals here. Ramos Angelis, one of his friends, spotted him.

"Chavis, amigo! Qué pasa?" greeted Ramos.

"Ramos!" said Chavis. He pointed toward the cockpit. "Look. You won't believe these cocks. I saw them fight in Franklin. That's why I'm here tonight. I'm following them! They're invincible!" The betting and bantering were warming up as wagers were called out loud and accepted by others. Johnny Bohannon proudly held up his contender.

"You gonna bet on this fight?" asked Ramos, whose cash was burning in his pocket.

"Well, kind of," Chavis answered over the chaotic roar of the crowd. "Twenty-five dollars on Diablo! Diablo, twenty-five!" he called out, waving his bills in the air. He was betting on the roundhead's opponent.

"Sí! Got your twenty-five!" came an answer.

"What?" said Angelis. "I thought you said they were great!"

"Strategy," said Chavis softly, with a wink. His hand with cash shot up again. "I got another twenty dollars for Diablo! Twenty for Diablo!"

"Okay. Got you, twenty dollars!"

The bidding continued after the cocks squared off. The contender birds were held out face-to-face to trigger their aggression, igniting their natural drive to subdue other male birds. Their necks fully extended, their feathers flared out, and their eyes sparkling with intensity. The battle began, and they leapt and lunged feet first at each other. Bohannon's roundhead was not as quick as his opponent and promptly suffered a gaff spearing. His movements weakened with repeated stabbings, and in a mere three minutes, he fell in defeat. The roar of the fans climaxed, followed by scuffling to settle wagers.

"What's this?" asked Ramus. "You said these birds were good. This was a slaughter!"

"Yeah," answered Chavis, milling through the crowd to collect his winnings. Then he pulled Ramus aside. "That bird was a punch cock, a runt. Now there'll be higher bets *against* the roundheads."

"Okay," Ramus said, envying the roll of bills in Chavis's hand.

"It may be better if we split up to bet. Just watch me. I'll see you after the derby's over."

"Sure. Thanks!"

John Bohannon tossed his losing bird's carcass into the trash barrel behind the pit in apparent disgust. The victor was held high before the cheering crowd. He was a Claret, with a larger, more triangular-shaped head. "Diablo!" announced his proud owner.

Bohannon produced another roundhead rooster, offering a challenge to the winner. Many laughed at this arrogant proposition after the opening match massacre.

"Tempest!" cried Bohannon. "We challenge Diablo!"

"One hundred dollars on Diablo!" called the first wager.

"Two hundred dollars on Diablo!" shouted another. These bets were met, hesitantly, by others. Ramus followed Chavis's lead, accepting bets for Tempest against Diablo. The gambling grew more lively than in the first fight.

In the cockpit, the owners readied their birds for battle. After a few starter lunges, collars of feathers raised around the roosters' heads, they were released. Tempest, the roundhead, was all muscle. His chest was flatter than the defending champ, and he was quick and strong. The cocks sparred, claws spread, stabbing at each other. This roundhead bird was nothing like his predecessor. He was fast, powerful, and precise—striking his opponent with bayonet-like stabs. Diablo posed a solid contest but could not land a piercing blow. Tempest remained untouched. The match lasted nearly ten minutes before Tempest strutted around his fallen foe.

The impressive fighting of Tempest had energized the crowd. Bills were exchanged in lively manner as two losing gamblers fled the barn to evade their creditors. The evening saw Tempest challenged four more times, and he finished as the derby champion with not a drop of his own blood shed. Chavis met Ramus outside the barn after the final match.

"How'd you do?" he asked.

"Probably close to a thousand dollars!" said Ramus with a grin, glancing about to assure no undesirables heard him.

"Wanna score some coke?" offered Chavis.

"Nah," he declined. "I've got some beers in my cooler. Want one?"

"Maybe, but I think I'll get some blow first. I'll see you, amigo."

"Sure. Thanks, amigo."

Chavis had spotted Skeeter and walked off toward him. Behind the barn, José dragged out the barrel of the dead losing roosters. He sprinkled gasoline on the spoils and lit them afire. The flames reflecting in Skeeter's eyes gave him a satanic look as he tendered his wares.

Dale Gregory drove along the dark country road between Chase City and Clarksville. His headlights showed a mound on the right shoulder ahead, partially blocking his lane. As he braked, he recognized it to be a dead deer, the victim of a hit and run. He pulled over to drag the carcass out of the roadway and noted the only obvious injury was to the head. The animal was warm and limp, freshly killed, with undamaged meat. If it was skinned and dressed tonight, the February weather still cold, it could make good venison. Even if not cleaned promptly, it could feed some dogs for a week. He decided to load the animal into his truck bed. The doe seemed about 110 pounds, a good size.

That week, Dr. Hardy had his office schedule interrupted by an urgent case. Lucy had put Hank in the office procedure room.

"Well, what's up?" asked Hardy.

"Ah, it's kinda embarrassing, Doc," Hank began, leaning forward to ensure the door was closed. "I've had this scar tissue on my penis for years. Just recently, it's become painful to have sex." He lowered his voice and continued. "I don't want anyone to know, not even Lucy."

"Sure. Of course."

"Well, it was just a small scar under the head. So I thought I'd just snip it with some scissors."

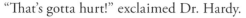

"That's gotta hurt!" exclaimed Dr. Hardy.

"Yeah ... but I can't stop the bleeding now!"

"Let's have a look."

Hank disrobed, and Dr. Hardy examined his manhood. There was a cut under the penile head from which red blood was oozing. Hank had a washcloth and toilet tissue in his underwear, heavily colored by blood. "I can numb this up and finish clipping the adhesion band—that is, the scar tissue."

"Okay. Do whatever you need to do. Just don't list this on a billing statement or anything. Darlene doesn't know about this. She was complaining that I had lost interest in sex. She wanted me to get some Viagra or something."

Dr. Hardy completed his delicate procedure and wrote "neck laceration" on the billing sheet. *It was just below the head, after all,* he thought. "You'll need the stitches out in six to seven days."

"I'll let *you* do that, Doc."

Shortly after his departure, Lucy brought Hank's billing sheet to Dr. Hardy. "What's this 'neck laceration'? He told me he had a problem with his *ear!*"

"Well, it was a little below the ear," fudged Hardy.

"Oh. Well, he didn't get us too far behind schedule 'cause Josh Nichols didn't show for his appointment."

Obie Hardy knew that Josh's transportation wasn't all that dependable. Several people had reported giving him rides home or to town. Mike Crawford had told Obie about one day finding Josh walking along the highway toward town on his prosthetic leg. He had pulled over to offer him a lift, and Josh came sprinting up to the car.

"Josh," Mike said, "I believe you can outrun me with your one leg!"

"Well, Craw-dad," Josh answered, "you never were that fast."

Dr. Hardy said to Lucy, "Maybe we should call him to reschedule. He has transportation problems sometimes."

"Yeah," she answered. "Loren called, but there was no answer. She left him a message."

It was three days later when Dr. Hardy received the call from the sheriff's office. They needed an ME at the ridge, three miles east of town on Route 58. His office had just closed for the day, but at five thirty in late February, it was dusk. The doctor recognized the house, set a ways back from the highway, with a well-worn black pickup truck in the yard. This was Josh Nichols's place.

Wilt Morris was the on-scene investigator. He led Dr. Hardy through the living room, littered with shotgun shell casings, jars of shot pellets of varying sizes, and a few engine parts.

"No one had seen him for two days," Wilt began. "His brother-in-law saw him here, at home, then. Neighbors were fishing in the pond beside the house yesterday and said he didn't come out and greet them. He usually does."

"Has he been ill?" asked Hardy. "He missed his appointment three days ago."

"The family reported that he complained of severe leg cramps. He'd had similar symptoms before when his blood sugars were high."

Josh's body was in the hall between the bedroom and the bathroom, facing up. His head was pointed toward the bathroom, and his artificial leg was not attached. His skin was cold, and full rigor mortis was present. There were bruises on his knees, presumably from crawling on the floor before dying. Hardy noted that the corpse looked dry, with sunken eye sockets and abdomen. He thought that a urine sample might help identify diabetic ketoacidosis. With a long needle, he made two attempts to withdraw urine, stabbing above the pubic area, but was unsuccessful.

"Bladder's empty, and he looks dry," stated Dr. Hardy. "It appears that he's dehydrated." He knew this was common with excessive blood sugar, or hyperglycemia. The eye fluid was in a relatively isolated body compartment and changed slowly in response to body chemistry changes. It was protected from the early changes of decay. It wouldn't reveal the immediate glucose reading at the time of death, but it would show how it was running for the hours before. As he extracted the thick, clear vitreous, he thought aloud. "Funny. He's had diabetes most of his life. He knew how to manage it." Other illnesses, especially infections in the body, could make diabetes run rampant, but there were no signs of another ailment. The chronic foot infection had been cured by the amputation years ago, and the other leg looked normal. "Did you find his medicines?"

Wilt nodded. "Yeah. Some pills in the kitchen and insulin in the bathroom."

Dr. Hardy checked the prescription bottles. the antidepressant Paxil and three muscle relaxants—diazepam, Zanaflex, and quinine. The Paxil had helped dampen his phantom limb pain, the pain he sensed in his leg that had been removed. The nerved fibers carrying messages to the spinal cord had become irritable after their sensory endings had been cut off. They would fire randomly, causing painful sensations that seemed to be in the missing appendage. The muscle relaxers were for the cramps that the family had reported.

Next, he looked at the insulin on the bathroom shelf. Josh was not out of insulin. There was about one-fourth of a vial remaining.

"Oh, yeah," noted Morris. "There's some insulin in the refrigerator, too."

"Okay. I'm going to call Richmond and present this case." Dr. Hardy called from the scene. The central office investigator felt that the death of a forty-seven-year-old diabetic with obvious disease complications constituted a "natural" death from the effects of his disease.

Dr. Hardy drove back to his office to organize the paperwork. He did have samples of blood and vitreous to send. Still, he felt an uncertainty. He took a tiny drop of the vitreous fluid and tested it on his office glucose meter. It read "HI," or over 600. Normal blood sugars run in the low 100s. Surely with the symptoms of leg cramps and an insulin supply available, Josh would have known what to do. And when he continued to worsen, he would have called for help. Dr. Hardy remembered Josh's hatred for the commonwealth attorney, Paul Mathis, and the mysterious fire only a few weeks earlier. *What if he was involved and someone tried to shut him up?* he wondered. *What if he knew about fire bombs or even made one?* He quickly called the sheriff's office and asked for Wilt Morris.

"Morris here."

"It's Dr. Hardy. Look, I have a hunch. Could you send the insulin bottle from Josh Nichols's bathroom to the forensics lab?"

"I guess so. But why?"

"Josh had diabetes most of his life. He knew what to do when his sugars were high. If someone tampered with his insulin, it could have contributed to his death."

"Okay. But why would someone do that?"

"It could be related to the Goode Building arson," he proposed.

"All right. But I don't know," said Morris, not yet aware of Josh's hobbies. "It seems like a long shot."

"Thanks. He was a friend of mine."

Underground | 10

DETECTIVE BRUCE DUFFER SAT AT his work desk in the sheriff's office, reviewing his mail. The desk was a plain, steel type with a laminate surface. A report from Consolidated Labs in Richmond caught his interest—it contained the fire investigation results from the Goode Building case. He wasn't surprised to see that they confirmed his field test findings for hydrocarbon accelerants, but the napthenate and palmitate compounds identified were unusual. He lifted a reference book from his desk drawer. The extensive listing of volatile chemicals was a publication of the National Fire Protection Association, NFPA Document 921. He studied the index briefly and then exclaimed aloud, "Napalm!"

He Googled "napalm" on his desk PC to research it. Napalm was used extensively in Korea and Vietnam for firebombing villages and enemy camps. It caused a prolonged, hot burning and stuck like tar to its target, including human flesh. Duffer found its use here odd, raising his suspicions that the arsonist had a military background. His cell phone rang, interrupting his thoughts.

"Yeah. Duffer here," he answered.

"Bruce, this is Wilt Morris. Can you come out to the Ridge? You know a lot about firearms and explosives, so I need you to see this!"

"Okay. I'm on my way."

He was given a familiar address, Josh Nichols's. He also knew that Josh did shotgun shell reloads and black powder hunting. They had probably found a barrel of gun powder and needed confirmation and advice on what to do with it.

When Duffer pulled up, Wilt met him in the driveway.

"So, did you find a powder keg?" asked Bruce Duffer.

"Well, yeah. But that's not the half of it!" He motioned to the woods behind the house. "Come on back here." At the edge of the woods there were double doors into the hillside, like the entrance to a storm cellar. Pulling open the doors, he continued, "The family found this, and we cut the padlocks for them."

It opened into a cinder block–lined bunker with, expectedly, two powder kegs but, additionally, some military-type weapons. Detective Wilt Morris called out the inventory. "Two gun powder kegs, three bazookas, an AK-47 automatic rifle, one dozen grenades, ten cases of rifle rounds, shotgun shells, and two gasoline jugs."

"Oh my god!" exclaimed Duffer. He noted they were about one hundred yards from the house, and there was a sewer-type vent pipe through the top of the bunker. "He placed this a safe distance from his house. He knew how dangerous it was to store explosives and volatiles in his residence."

"Oh," added Morris, "and there's some packs of styrofoam cups, too. I guess he used them when entertaining his arms-dealing clients."

"Possibly. He also may have used them with the gasoline to make napalm," Duffer speculated, remembering a home recipe from fire school. "A coincidence?"

"Coincidence? What?"

"Never mind. I just found that napalm traces were in the forensics from the Goode Building arson. I was just thinking out loud."

Dr. Hardy stopped by Tanner Funeral Home after hospital rounds

Wednesday morning. All bodies scheduled for cremation required a viewing by the ME, to avert obvious destruction of evidence. He reviewed the death certificate and remains of the seventy-two-year-old man who had died two weeks after having heart bypass surgery.

"Can we remove the pacemaker?" asked Betty Tanner, owner of the funeral home.

"Well, sure," answered Hardy. "What do you do with it?" He imagined it could be sterilized and donated to a developing country for reuse.

"We return them to the manufacturer. If it's a defibrillator, they send someone to deactivate it before we handle the body."

A good safety practice, thought Hardy. "So do these have a lifetime warranty?" he jested.

"I don't know about that. But they explode when we cremate the body. It's dangerous."

"I didn't realize that."

"Yeah. The furnace temperature has to reach sixteen hundred degrees. We're looking into getting a unit here in town. Currently, we send them to Lawrenceville. It creates about a one-day delay," Mrs. Tanner explained.

Dr. Hardy removed his gloves after surveying the body. There were no bruises, fractures, knife wounds, or bullet holes. He signed the one-page form and handed it to Betty Tanner. "Here you go."

"Thanks, Dr. Hardy."

When the doctor arrived at his office, Lucy had the first morning patients in the exam rooms. "You may want to see *your* suture removal in the procedure room while I draw blood in room 1," she said.

"Okay," he said, entering the procedure room. It was Hank, the penile "neck" laceration. "This has healed well," reported Hardy, as he removed the two stitches. "Is it still painful when aroused?"

"No, sir, Doc," said Hank with a smile. "It is itching some, 'though."

Itching for action, thought Hardy. "That's natural. It's the healing process. I hope all goes well. Take care."

"Thanks, Doc."

At lunch, Lucy had the local *News Progress* paper. "They think the Goode Building was arson," she said. A picture of Sheriff Larrimore, cowboy hat on, headed the article. "The site analysis and forensics point to an intentional cause of the fire."

"Well, we thought that all along," said Dr. Hardy. "Paul Mathis, the commonwealth attorney, had his office in there. I'm sure he's made some dangerous enemies."

"Oh, Obie," said Lucy, still studying the paper. "They've passed the dog leash law in town. Effective July 1."

"Crap! We've gotta get us a place out of town! It's not right to keep dogs restrained. It makes them hyper and aggressive when let loose. Maybe we can find some land near the lake."

"You've been saying that for years."

"Well, it's time to shit or get off the pot."

The afternoon brought a young, black, male patient with a "personal problem" listed as his complaint.

"And what problems are you having?" asked Dr. Hardy.

"I got the drip," he said. "My girlfriend says she was treated for clinama."

"Are you running any fever?" Hardy asked, assuming "clinama" might be chlamydia.

"No, but I'm sore in my limp glands," he said, pointing to his groins. "I thought I might need some erector-mycin or something."

Dr. Hardy inserted a tiny cotton swab into his penile opening for a lab specimen.

"Whoa, shit!" he exclaimed.

"Sorry. At least it's quick," Hardy stated, placing the swab into the sampling tube. "Do you use condoms?"

"Sometimes. But I don't always strap up."

Dr. Hardy decided to give antibiotics to cover the ubiquitous gonorrhea and chlamydia and wrote out the prescriptions. "Condoms help prevent the twelve STDs," advised Hardy. "Thirteen, if you count pregnancy." Dr. Hardy felt that the medical condition, pregnancy, could cause maternal health problems, require surgery (a C-section), or even be fatal and should qualify as a "disease." It too was sexually transmitted from male to female, and the male could also be affected via eighteen years of child support.

Lorene met Dr. Hardy in the hallway after the appointment. "There's an ME case in Finchley," she said.

Hardy sighed. "Okay, I can get back within an hour. Offer for us to see the patients who will wait. Otherwise, reschedule them."

"Okay. Will do."

Dr. Hardy knew that Lorne was good at handling disruptions in the office routine. He trusted her almost as much as Lucy.

As Dr. Hardy drove across the bridge at Butcher's Creek, he looked across the lake. The water sparkled in the early afternoon sun. Yes, it was time to find a place on the lake. He could talk to some realtors and see if there were any good buys available. The next intersection was his turn, Sullivan Road. He followed that road to the scene.

The location was a new home site. Investigator Wilt Morris met him in the driveway. "It's over here, down the hill," he directed. "It's a little muddy. They were digging the septic and drain field."

Two rescue workers stood with Dale Gregory beside the body. Gregory was the contractor for the job. The dead man lay on the dirt alongside the ditch, which appeared about seven to eight feet deep. The excavated dirt was piled up along the opposite edge of the ditch, effectively creating a bank wall twelve to fourteen feet high.

"He was working on the pipe down there," stated the EMT, pointing to the deepest point in the ditch. "The backhoe operator saw it collapse."

"The backhoe operator is his cousin," added Morris.

"Yeah," said Gregory. "He was probably buried about ten minutes.

His cousin had to dig off the dirt until we could reach him. But ... he wasn't breathing when we pulled him out." Gregory held his hand to his forehead, shielding his eyes from the sunlight, as if that was the cause of his watering eyes.

"They were working for Gregory, here," noted Detective Morris.

The body was that of a Hispanic male, age nineteen, slender at about 150 pounds. Dr. Hardy initially suspected that he had suffocated beneath the soil. He looked under his shirt and found multiple chest bruises and felt a right clavicle fracture. There was no air palpable underneath the skin, which would have indicated a punctured lung. Blood oozed from the nose and ears, signs of fractures in the base of the skull. The right jaw was also broken, and a large bruise covered his right temple and forehead. There was excessive mobility of the neck when Dr. Hardy maneuvered the head. Last, Hardy placed his plastic thermometer in the armpit.

"The cause of death was definitely a crush injury. The head and neck are more damaged than the chest," Dr. Hardy summarized. "I don't think suffocation was the problem. He probably was unconscious and died quickly."

"OSHA [Occupational Safety and Health Administration] will need to be contacted," said Morris, "since he was on a job."

"I'm sure the Richmond office will do an autopsy for that reason, as well," said Hardy. As he stepped back from the body, the mud under his shoes pulled back against him.

Dale Gregory stood silent. He used these men part time for projects, often paying them in cash. They were cheap labor. Since he was not officially their employer, their immigration status had not been validated. The potential repercussions from OSHA and possibly Immigration could be overwhelming. Hopefully, the family members would downplay the extent of his hiring them as unverified laborers.

"Do we have a name?" asked Dr. Hardy, as he retrieved his thermometer.

"Ramos Angelis," stated Detective Morris.

Final Arrangements | 11

DETECTIVE BRUCE DUFFER HAD ANOTHER clandestine meeting with undercover agent Randy Stephens, aka "Danny Hanes," at the interstate rest area in Bracey, just north of the North Carolina border. Stephens reported that he had followed Skeeter on a Sunday, two weeks earlier. He had turned onto Red Lawn Road and then abandoned the tail to avoid exposure. The next Sunday afternoon, he had staged a flat tire on Route 4 near the Red Lawn Road intersection. His undercover beard had proved beneficial because the February breeze was a little chilly, especially since he had to hold his position for some time. Finally, he spotted Skeeter turning again onto Red Lawn Road at about 4:00 p.m. He resumed his pursuit.

Arriving at the chicken barn shortly behind Skeeter, Stephens surveyed the scene. Skeeter Richards stationed himself outside, so agent Stephens entered the barn. There were about eighty to one hundred people packed inside the barn, of various ethnicities and races—Hispanic, Filipino, black, and white. Many appeared to be farmworkers and probably were associated with the fowl livestock there.

The cool winter air was warmed by the crowd, the cigar smoke, and a wood stove near the concession counter.

"Ten dollars," said the door girl. Stephens produced his cover charge and entered.

The crowd buzzed with anticipatory excitement. The pit was empty, as the derby had yet to begin. Some contenders held their cocks in their arms while even more animals were caged. Stephens saw that he had stumbled onto something quite different from drug distribution activities. When the spectators began calling out bets, he blended in to avert suspicion.

"Twenty dollars on Demonio!" he shouted above the growing noise.

"Got your twenty," answered a slender, young Hispanic man.

Stephens heard someone nearby call the man who'd accepted his bet Ramos. Now he was gambling! It was a ploy to protect his cover, but nonetheless, it was an illegal activity. He was caught up in the cesspool of the derby. There was, however, excitement. The din of the crowd, the challenge of the cockfight, the thrill of wagering—this was far more entertaining than playing bingo or scratching a lottery ticket. But illegal gambling was still a crime, and it was hypocritical to break the law trying to apprehend lawbreakers. So his involvement would be limited to making payments for information, prohibiting him from collecting on bets. This took the fun out of winning but let him maintain some element of integrity.

Ramos found him after Demonio had been beaten. "Twenty dollars, por favor," he asked.

Stephens handed him a twenty, making good on his information purchase. To maximize the value, he began milling about. He approached the concession stand.

"Got any beer?" he asked.

"No alcohol inside the barn," stated the overweight black woman at the counter. This was an interesting rule, a bit of etiquette among this corruption.

"Are the hot dogs beef?"

"Chicken!" she said, grinning slyly, a gold star inlay in her incisor shining.

He had just witnessed the losing rooster being tossed into a barrel. "Okay, then. I'll take a burger and a Coke," he said.

He wandered outside while eating to explore further. He spotted Laymar Richards, "Skeeter," standing by a tree. His left pant leg cuff was rolled up a bit. Stephens recognized this as an urban street signal that he had drugs available. Stephens didn't know the identity of the stout black man standing just behind Skeeter. He looked like he could be a bouncer and was most likely protection for the drug dealer, probably armed. Stephens wandered about for a short time before taking leave. He didn't risk wearing out his welcome.

"So," Stephens reported to Duffer at their meeting, "on Sundays, this Laymar Richards sets up shop at the cockfight barn out on Red Lawn Road! Easily a hundred people there."

"Cockfights?" asked Duffer.

"Yep. Well organized too, with a cover charge, refreshments, and open gambling."

"Aren't cockfights legal?"

"Well, in Virginia, they actually are legal. It is, however, illegal to charge admission and to bet on the outcome."

"Sure!"

"And of course, the drug sales are frowned upon by the law, too."

"Obviously. Hence, Laymar."

"I looked into cockfighting. It's a common pastime in Mexico, the Philippines, and other countries. The Sunday afternoon fights. Just like seeing a movie, or a ball game, or playing bingo here. It's part of our American heritage, too. The betting adds to the excitement but isn't an essential part. I found this magazine in the trash there." Stephens handed Duffer a publication. "It could hold some fingerprints or just some information on the magnitude of this activity."

"Sure," said Duffer. "*Grit and Steel.* I've never heard of it."

Agent Stephens had acquired a cursory knowledge of cockfighting history since attending the fight and shared what he knew with Duffer.

Dating back to 400 BC, the spectacle had entertained royalty to riffraff. In some countries, the fighting area, or cockpit, was the center for the town marketplace. One nation reported tax revenues from cockfighting activities were second only to tobacco. American forefathers who relished it included George Washington, Andrew Jackson, Henry Clay, and Benjamin Franklin. Even Abraham Lincoln defended the sport when a movement to abolish cockfighting was starting. Contemporary poultry farms keep thousands of chickens crammed into crowded cages and feed them hormone-enhanced feed to maximize their growth until they reach the slaughter age of six months. Breed cocks, on the other hand, have spacious pens, are fed premium diets, and receive vaccinations. They live a long, full life if they are winners, giving them a 50 percent chance, compared to the 100 percent six-month mortality of their fryer siblings. The honor, respect, and dignity a champion fighter cock achieves are an impossibility for typical farmed fowl, riding in the fast lane to their fast food destiny.

"Well," commented Duffer, "cockfighting's merits aside, the activity attracts shady crowds. You've seen drugs and gambling there already. What's next? Prostitution? Assaults? Murder? I don't want my kids around that!"

"True. Anyway, we will need a coordinated effort of multiple disciplines to blow this out of the water."

"Yeah. Sure. I'll get this to Sheriff Larrimore."

"Good. I'm ready to get this stuff done. Some of it's a little scary."

"I don't envy your job," Duffer concluded as he stood to leave. A detective's job was stressful enough. Undercover agents were like their special forces soldiers. "Be careful, and we'll be in touch."

"Sure thing. Thanks."

Dale Gregory approached the registration desk at the dental office in Clarksville. "I need to get some dental records from one of my workers," he stated. "Ramos Angelis. He had a tooth pulled here about six months ago."

"Oh, yes," said the receptionist. "I think you paid his bill, right?"

"Yeah, that's right. He was missing work because of that tooth."

"What's his problem now?"

"He was killed in an accident last week. I need the records for the medical examiner's office. He suffered facial injuries, and they need to verify his identity."

"Oh, I'm so sorry. He was a nice patient. I'll get that record for you right now."

"Okay. Thank you."

Dale Gregory carried the small manila envelope back to his truck. Later, he called Dr. Hardy to proffer this data.

"Thanks, Mr. Gregory," said Dr. Hardy, "but I think they used the witness's verifications of his identity. If I find out that we need those records, I'll get back in touch."

"Okay, Doc. Whatever you say."

Dr. Hardy had just received the forensics report on Josh Nichols from Consolidated Labs. As he expected, the vitreous glucose level was high—936—meaning that his blood glucose had been even higher, probably over 1,000! A blood reading from the body would have been useless because of the deterioration of the blood by the time the specimens were drawn and, further, the time required for transportation to the lab by mail. Also, with prolonged time after death, fermentation consumes the sugars. The more interesting finding was from the insulin bottle analysis. It was found to contain 99.3 percent water, with only a trace amount—0.7 percent—of human insulin. Hardy immediately phoned investigator Wilt Morris. Wilt had received his forensics report as well.

"So what's this mean?" asked Morris.

"His insulin bottle was filled with *water*! Josh was not able to lower his blood sugar since he was injecting himself with water instead of insulin! If someone intentionally replaced his insulin with water, that would be murder. Right?" explained Hardy.

"Hmm," said Morris, reflecting on the munitions bunker and Bruce Duffer's comment about the Goode Building. "Thanks. We'll look into this a little further."

Dale Gregory continued his efforts to help with Ramos Angelis's arrangements. He had been a good worker whom Dale had assisted before, and Dale now felt driven to help this final time. Ramos had literally given his life for Dale's contracted job. Whether out of respect for this laborer, guilt that he had died on this project, or fear of OSHA prosecution, Dale Gregory longed to somehow make it right. The family wished that his remains be returned to Mexico. But the cost of a fifteen hundred–mile hearse transport and embalming would be astronomical. Dale had arranged to meet with Maxwell Walker, the funeral director of Maxwell Walker Funeral Home and Crematory in Clarksville.

"I'm helping the Angelis family," he explained. "They can't afford to get the body back to Mexico."

"I understand," noted Maxwell. Maxwell Walker was a tall, lean man with short black hair, and he appeared comfortable in a suit and tie. His movements were smooth and sure, his manner courteous. "I might suggest you consider cremation as an option. We can perform that service here and forgo embalming and casket expenses."

"That sounds good."

"And they can carry the ash remains themselves. There'd be no need for body transportation. Now, are they Catholic? I know many Hispanics are."

"I don't know," said Dale. "Why?"

"Historically, Catholicism has frowned upon cremations. But since John F. Kennedy Jr. was cremated seven years ago, it has been viewed almost equally with traditional burials. I can discuss this with the family."

"All right," said Dale, a little relieved. "If they agree to that, I'll pay for his expenses."

"Very good, Mr. Gregory. Would you like to see our cremation furnace in the back?"

"Yeah, sure. That would be interesting."

"I have some urns and water dispersal floats on display back there, too." Maxwell was clearly proud of his crematorium, the most recent addition to his business, and was eager to promote it. "Incidentally, in the past, the state required embalming and a casket for cremations. That didn't save much on funeral expenses. Now we can cremate without embalming or a casket, if the cremation can be performed promptly."

"Well, this certainly is an asset to our community," stated Dale as he looked over the large furnace in the preparatory room.

The next day found Dr. Hardy in the prep room in the back of Maxwell Walker Funeral Home. He had been asked to sign the cremation form for Ramos Angelis, since the decision to cremate had been made after the body had returned from the Richmond ME's office.

"Thanks, Dr. Hardy. I appreciate you doing this," said Max. "The ME's office would fax me a signed one, but I wouldn't have the usual triplicate copies." He fired the burner while he spoke. "I'll just start this up. It takes sixteen to eighteen minutes to reach the proper temperature. The family is in my office now."

"Okay," said Hardy, handing Max the three carbonless copies.

As Hardy left, he noticed Dale Gregory in his pickup truck outside the rear entrance. They waved at each other. Dr. Hardy smiled to think that this devoted employer had driven the family to the funeral home. There might be some silver lining to this dark cloud.

The memorial service was held at the Catholic Church in Clarksville, four doors down from the funeral home. Dale was part of the sparse congregation made up largely of Hispanics. A brief smile crossed his face as he wondered why the service wasn't entirely in Spanish. He recognized José Mortez among the mourners and spoke with him after the service.

"José, it's been a long time."

"Sí. Ramos was a good man and a friend."

"Yeah. It was awful, the cave-in."

"I know," José said, shaking his head. "If you need my help for anything, you can call me. I will help any way I can."

"Thanks, José."

Ramos's cousin approached Dale, holding the cremation urn. "Here is our address in Mexico. We will take Ramos home. I'm not sure when we may come back."

Dale wondered whether their presence in the States was legal and whether Immigration was after them.

"You can reach me if you need to," the cousin said.

"Thanks," Dale said, taking the folded paper he was offered.

"No. Thank you, amigo, for all your help."

He nodded, sincerely.

Dr. Hardy's next ME call was from the South Hill hospital. A man who had died in the ER was a prisoner, requiring a mandatory investigation. He examined the body around noon, still in the ER. Gary Sloan was a sixty-seven-year-old black man with a history of a past heart attack, or myocardial infarction. He had reported chest pains beginning at 7:00 a.m., had arrived at the prison infirmary at 11:00 a.m., and had promptly collapsed. An automatic defibrillator had been used, delivering a series of three shocks, after which the nursing staff started CPR. By the time the EMTs delivered the decedent to the ER, he had been unconscious for fifty-two minutes. The cardiac monitor showed he had flatlined, asystole. He was deemed a DOA—dead on arrival.

Dr. Hardy's examination revealed a middle-aged, medium-built man in prison jeans and boots. He had a mustache, a warm body temperature at 92.7 degrees, and no evidence of bruising or bone fractures. All evidence was consistent with a coronary death, by natural causes. The central office investigator agreed to an autopsy since the fatality had occurred under incarceration. The state required proof that deaths of prisoners were not a result of their confinement.

As usual, it was six weeks before Dr. Hardy received the autopsy report. The inmate's cause of death was now officially atherosclerotic cardiovascular disease. The heart muscle was thickened, a consequence of high blood pressure, and all three coronary arteries had blockages of 80 to 90 percent.

The same week, the results on Ramos Angelis came in the mail. Some findings struck Dr. Hardy as odd. He had a Mexican identification card on him under a different name with a photograph that did not resemble Ramos. There was $1,523 in cash in his pockets. His toxicology reports showed that he was drug-free. His exam had revealed multiple skull fractures with extensive subarachnoid hemorrhages—bleeding around the surface of the brain, which had been determined to be the cause of death. Some bruising of the lungs was also present. Dr. Hardy wondered about his immigration status, given the bogus ID, and about the large amount of money he was carrying, possibly unreported cash wages.

Patient Sheila Long later arrived in Dr. Hardy's office for her thyroid function test.

"You know I'm selling real estate full-time now," she said as Dr. Hardy wrote her prescription.

"Really? How's that going?" he asked.

"Pretty good. Properties move well around the lake."

"Oh. That reminds me. I'm actually looking for a good deal on some lake property. We want to move out of town."

"Sure. You can cut down on your taxes, too."

"And no dog leash laws," he added.

"Are you interested in Gaston or Buggs Island?" she asked, referring to the lakes on both sides of the dam.

"Probably Buggs Island. We'd like to be close to Boydton, to the office. And we'd like at least five acres—room for a big yard and for the dog to run."

"I think we have some acreage toward Eagle Point. I'll get you the map and specs on it."

"Great." His family had farmland in that area already. It sounded promising. He handed her the prescription. "I'll let you know if this medicine dose needs adjusting when your labs come back."

Plans | 12

It was dusk as Dale Gregory returned home. He was still finishing the new home on Sullivan Road where the sewage ditch had caved in. It still weighed heavily on his mind. An OSHA investigator had called and made an inquiry but felt a site visit was unnecessary. That had lightened the burden somewhat. As he walked up his porch steps, he noticed a paper taped to his door. It was from the county sheriff's office. He carried it inside to read in the light.

The notice was a court summons, a debt claim from Bank of America for a MasterCard account with a $28,683 balance and a Visa card balance of $16,834, for a total of $45,517. The court date was July 13, 2006, at 9:00 a.m. Dale was numb at first, like the strength had bled from his body. He started to have a fine tremor, which intensified as his adrenalin surged, and finally, full-blown anger emerged. *Sarina!* he thought. *What a selfish bitch!*

"Sarina!" he screamed into the vacant house. "Sarina!" There was no answer. He panicked, pacing about the kitchen, thoughts running wild.

Two beers hadn't squelched his rage significantly when Sarina finally arrived. He met her at the front door. "What the hell is this?" he cried, waving the summons in front of her.

"What?" she countered.

"Nearly fifty thousand dollars in credit card bills! What were you thinking?"

"I don't know. This can't be right!" she babbled. She didn't need to read the papers for she knew what was brewing.

"Well, I canceled the cards two weeks ago. The interest accumulates every day!" He turned away from her and stepped back and then charged toward her again. "You'll take *years* to pay this off with your Peebles store job!"

"Me? My job? I don't think so!"

"Think again, missy! I'm not going down from this!"

"Well, I don't have to take this crap! *You* deal with it! I'm outta here!" She turned around and stormed back out of the door, slamming it behind her. Dale started after her, opening the door but stopping on the porch.

"Sarina!" he yelled. "You come back here!" He realized as he said it that this was not what he really wanted right now.

"No way! I've had enough of this shit!" She jerked the door of her Saturn closed and threw gravel from her tires as she raced away. Dale kicked the post of the porch and then limped back inside. He needed another beer.

The following day, Dale went over to his parents' home to share his emotional and financial plight with them. He was a little groggy from little sleep and lots of alcohol.

"I don't know what to do! I've been working my ass off, and Sarina's been sucking us dry!" he ranted.

"Is there anything I can do to help?" his father asked sympathetically. He was known for his soft-spoken manner and usually projected an honest wisdom.

"I don't know. If you gave me money, she'd end up with it. I don't want her to get another penny!"

"What about your equipment?"

"I wouldn't be able to work without it. The tractor's paid for. I still owe on the backhoe," said Dale.

His father thought quietly for a few minutes and then made a proposal. "What if I bought your equipment, took over the payments, and 'leased it' to you? Then they might not be able to get at it." Dale rubbed his chin, pondering this option. He wasn't accustomed to business wheeling and dealing, but now his back was against the wall. This strategy appeared to be the most reasonable choice.

"Okay. That might be the answer," he conceded.

Sheriff Clay Larrimore had assembled Bruce Duffer and Wilt Morris in his office to meet with Bob Walden from the Virginia State Police. After introductions, Larrimore closed the door and began.

"We've named this investigation 'Grit and Steel.' Our undercover agent, following a drug-dealing suspect, uncovered this cockfighting operation. Although cockfighting itself is legal in Virginia, across the line in North Carolina, it's a felony. There are illegal gambling, more drugs, and possible illegal immigrants involved."

"You may well recall two men were shot dead in Texas last month," stated Detective Morris. "Their dispute was over a cockfight there."

"So who owns the cockfighting site?" Walden questioned. He was classic Virginia State Police, clean-cut, with a military look in the gray uniform with the Canadian Mountie-style hat.

"The property is registered to Logan Lumber Company, run by Paul Logan from Chase City," reported Morris.

"Does anyone live there?" asked Officer Walden.

"No, but a Mexican takes care of the property—José Mortez," continued Morris. He handed Walden a photo print from Mortez's driver's license.

"Cockfighting is popular with the Hispanics," added Walden. "Since it is illegal in North Carolina, it's not surprising that the site is less than fifteen miles from the state line. I suspect there are illegals involved. We'll need the departments of Immigrations and Homeland Security involved, but not up front."

"Sure, that's smart," said Sheriff Larrimore.

"What kind of time frame are we talking about?" asked Bruce Duffer.

"Well, to coordinate with the DEA and Immigrations, probably four to five months," Walden stated.

"Okay," said Larrimore. "Give us three days' to a week's notice before the bust. I can offer ten to twelve county officers for local support and backup."

"Fine. We'll be in touch. I'll plan for us to meet just before the strike," said Walden.

"All right."

"Now. We *must* have absolute secrecy for this to be successful," Walden emphasized. "No discussing this operation with *anyone*—spouses, friends, even fellow lawmen. Okay?"

"Sure," said Wilt Morris.

"Of course," agreed Duffer.

Duffer took Morris to meet with undercover agent Stephens in the dark, wee morning hours. It was a balmy July night, enriched by the crickets and the night bird calls.

Duffer introduced the two. "Wilt Morris here will be heading the investigation on our end. It's called Operation Grit and Steel," he said.

"We can't give out any details until the bust is set up," stated Morris.

"Yeah, sure," Stephens acknowledged. "Any idea as to when?"

"Maybe four to five months. We thank you for your recon info. Your work started all this."

"Good. I'm glad there's something positive to show from this job. Here are some names I've overheard of some patrons." He handed Morris a folded page of paper.

"All right, thanks," concluded Duffer as he stood, patting Stephens on the shoulder. "We'll be in touch."

Since she left Dale, Sarina Gregory had been staying at the Quality Inn in South Boston. Her lodging was being paid for by Brad, who, indeed, lodged with her there most nights. She got a discounted weekly rate, and it looked slightly better than her running straight to his place. She was, nonetheless, still married. When Brad arrived with their pizza and beer, she had a document in her hand.

"I've raised Dale's life insurance coverage to $250,000!" she said, cheerfully waving the papers. "And double that for an accidental death." She smiled at him. "Half a million! We could be on easy street!"

She appeared dead serious now. With the stakes this high, it became a more tempting proposition to Brad. She was Eve with the apple. Maybe if she were to just increase Dale's likelihood of a fatal "accident," that might not be true murder—just exposing him to a risk. Construction work actually was a dangerous occupation.

"Hmm," Brad pondered. "Does he know?"

"Of course not, silly. I paid the increased premium myself, so he won't be billed for at least six months." Her eyes were afire, but not from lust. Greed and a growing disgust for Dale were driving her now.

"I still don't think I can do anything to him, Sarina," stated Brad, almost apologetically. He did not have a violent nature. He was more of a good-time guy. And, adultery aside, he was not even a law breaker.

"Oh, you don't need to worry, honey," she said softly as she gently touched his neck and face. "I'll take care of everything. I might just need a little help from you. That's all, maybe not even that."

"The less I know about it, the better," he said.

"Oh, let's just forget about all that for now. Okay?" She stepped back and redirected the conversation. "That pizza smells so good!"

"Okay. Good. Let's eat." He reached first for a light beer. Sarina's plotting was unnerving, but, so far, it was just the talk of an embittered woman.

On Monday, Sheila Long stopped by Dr. Hardy's office. Her visit was not medical in nature; she was in real estate agent mode. She handed him an envelope in the hallway, between patients.

"Look this over. I've included some lots on the Skipwith road as well. The advantage is that they can qualify for dock permits. The acreage toward Eagle Point is protected, red-zoned." Hardy knew about the zoning codes that the Army Corps of Engineers assigned for the lake perimeter. The red meant no docks or mooring buoys. The intent was to preserve the natural beauty of the lake, in essence making it a national park.

"Great. I'll look them over," he said.

"You can clear a walkway to the lake in a red zone," she added.

"Oh, yeah?" He looked briefly at the plats. "Humph. The Eagle Point tract is priced at $120,000. That's $3,000 an acre for the forty acres. Farmland around here has been selling at a thousand or less an acre."

"I think the owner believes there's a lakefront development potential."

"Well, the tract is long and narrow, like a ribbon. Only five to ten acres on the narrow end would be lakefront. The rest should be priced like farmland. And there will be a long access road to maintain."

"Yeah. You're right. They also think there's forty to fifty thousand in timber on the property. Anyway, you can look it over and make an offer."

"Okay, I will," agreed Dr. Hardy. "I'll look over the Skipwith tracts, too."

"Great. I'll call you next week," said Sheila.

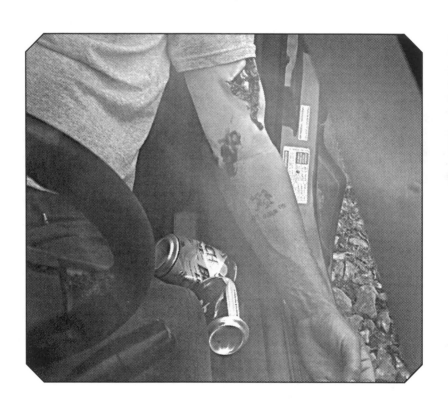

Unrestrained | 13

DALE GREGORY WAS SLUMPED ON his couch, lost in thought. He was pondering the options before him that might untangle his life. Sarina had abandoned him, a worker had been killed on the job, and creditors were calling him to court. The ringing telephone interrupted his thoughts.

"Hello," he answered flatly.

"Hello. I'm looking for Dale Gregory," greeted the caller.

"Speaking."

"Mr. Gregory, I'm an examiner with Southern Life. I need to get up with you for some blood work and a urine test."

"Okay. But why now?" asked Dale.

"I guess because you increased your coverage amount."

"Increased my coverage? What do you mean?"

"Didn't you just raise your coverage to $250,000?"

"No, I didn't. But …" He paused, suddenly remembering his furious wife. *Could Sarina be up to something?* he thought. "I guess my wife did. That's okay. Can we meet next week?"

"Sure. I can come to your house on Wednesday. Ten o'clock okay?"

"Yeah, sure. I can be here."

"Okay, fine. Oh, nothing to eat or drink for five to six hours before."

"All right. I'll see you then." *I'll certainly need to change my beneficiary!* he thought. *Could she be so evil as to plan to kill me?* Maybe she was just hedging her bets, in the event that the stress he was enduring might cause his demise. Maybe he could get a step ahead of her. He would surely be more careful now with a higher bounty on his head.

Dr. Hardy was paged as he pulled into his driveway. He had just finished his ten-hour workday when the "9-1-1" display on his beeper portended another task.

"We need an ME near Baskerville," announced the dispatcher. "A highway fatality, on Baskerville Road."

"Okay," said Hardy with a sigh, restarting his Jeep. "I can be there in ten to fifteen minutes."

An early dusk colored the autumn sky deep blue with crisp, purplish clouds, sharpened by the low humidity. As he drove up the long, straight hill on highway 58, he saw the blinking running lights of the Med Flight helicopter as it rose above the horizon. It passed over the road ahead of him, heading north toward the Medical College of Virginia, technically VCU Medical Center now. Turning south onto Baskerville Road, he saw the glow from his destination about a mile away. Blue police flashers, red ambulance lights, and orange tow truck lights pulsed brightly. The shimmering colors made the scene dance with excitement. Southside Rescue Squad had erected floodlights to illuminate the wreck site.

A Virginia state policeman was filing a highway fatality report, and Detective Bruce Duffer was assisting with evidence and documentation. Duffer addressed Hardy as the latter approached.

"The vehicles hit head on," Duffer said. He spoke loudly, to be heard above the noise from the lighting generator. "The driver of the

Chevrolet was alive, Med-Flighted out. The decedent is in the car beside the fence."

"The Chevrolet is in the left lane," noted Hardy. "Did that cause the wreck?"

"Not hardly. It was traveling in the opposite direction. It spun around 180 degrees on impact. The other driver was traveling about eighty miles per hour. His car was thrown from the road, over there." It was no wonder that this collision had been violent enough to kill.

"When did this happen?"

"A resident reported the crash was at 19:01. EMS was on the scene at 19:19 and found him dead."

"What's his name?" asked Dr. Hardy, pulling a clipboard from his medical examiner bag.

"Trooper Hite has the demographics," noted Duffer. He looked toward the state trooper who was approaching them.

"Alberto Samirez," stated the trooper. "Date of birth, 1-23-88." Holding out the driver's license, he continued. "It's not his car. I don't think he has a local address. He was unrestrained, but the air bags deployed. The force of the impact crushed the driver's compartment."

Dr. Hardy approached the vehicle off the right shoulder of the road. It rested in the line of a wooden fence, having knocked out a section of it. The front end was crushed in at an angle, bent deepest into the driver's area. It was a red Honda Civic with North Carolina license plates. The legs of the body were pinned under the dashboard, and the left arm was entangled in the twisted metal of the door. Under the passenger side of the dash, in a more protected area, was an opened twelve-pack box of beer with four cans missing. By now, darkness had fallen, and Dr. Hardy welcomed the artificial illumination, despite the loud roar of the generator.

He placed his thermometer in the left armpit and noted that the fractured humerus was protruding through a wound in the skin and that the jaw and chest had a total of five lacerations. He started palpating the body. Reaching under the dashboard, he identified broken bones in the right foot, left tibia (calf), and left femur (thigh). EMS workers had previously pried the metal away from driver's body somewhat, using their hydraulic wedge. Hardy checked his temperature reading: 88 degrees. The reading was consistent with this now being two hours after the crash.

Medical examiner Hardy noted an unusual tattoo on the left forearm. It was a black, outlined drawing of a bird holding a snake in his claw. Below the bird were the letters "eMe," bordered on each end by a cactus. He couldn't identify the bird; the features were not those of an eagle or other bird of prey.

"Bruce. Did you get a picture of this tattoo?" he asked.

"I think so, but we hadn't moved the body then. Hold out his arm, and I'll get a better shot."

"Okay," said Hardy, extending the appendage as the detective flashed two photographs.

"Got it," announced Duffer. The detective leaned over to take a closer look at the flesh artwork. The image of a bird tattoo in the midst of a cockfighting investigation was certainly curious. "Is that a rooster?" he posed.

"I don't think so," said Dr. Hardy. "The tail feathers point down, and there's no rooster comb."

"I see. Curious, 'though."

"Yeah."

Later, at his kitchen table, Dr. Hardy transferred his scene sketch of the forearm tattoo onto his CME-1 report form. Suddenly, he made the connection—the cactus and a snake-killing bird. It was a road runner! Coincidently, the man sporting the tattoo had died while running the road. Had the snake been a rattlesnake, it would have been more obvious. Hardy still wondered about the "eMe" lettering and whether it was some kind of gang logo. Anyway, it would not be relevant to this highway fatality but would be recorded in detail in his report.

"Obie!" called Lucy as she burst into the kitchen. "This was on our front door!" She slapped a paper on the table in front of him.

"What is it?" he asked, starting to read.

"A summons! We're being sued over our dog!"

"Huh?" He scanned the charges. "Violating the town ordinance ... about the leash law. I guess they're serious."

"What are we gonna do? We can't be sued. They'll wipe us out!"

"Who filed this?" he asked, starting to read.

"The mayor's wife! Sarah Gauldin! You'll have to go to court. I can't do this myself." She was boiling.

"Okay, sure. I'll schedule to take off that morning."

"Do we need to get a lawyer?" Lucy asked.

"I don't know. We'll see what fees could be involved. It may be too petty for all that," he said hopefully.

"Well, we can't keep Mickey if we're gonna be sued all the time."

"Oh, Lucy. That reminds me—I got some specs on some lake properties. We need to look at them and see if there are any good deals."

"Good. We'll need a big yard for the dog to run in," Lucy added.

"I know. One tract has forty acres, and it's not five miles from town."

"When can we see it?"

"Hopefully, this weekend."

That Saturday, Sheila Long drove the Hardys out on Taylor Ferry Road and turned onto a crude dirt drive.

"They gave me permission to use this farm road to show the property," Sheila explained, as she drove her red SUV slowly through a muddy puddle the size of a room. "Usually, just hunters use it. We'll still have to walk the last two hundred yards or so." Dr. Hardy smiled at Lucy. He longed for some wilderness, isolation from people who might regulate or control his home life.

They began their trek through a field in the adjoining farm to reach the lake perimeter boundary, marked by orange stripes painted on the trees.

"The property has six hundred feet of border along the Corps," she announced. That was the waterfront exposure.

"Well, there's a potential home site here," noted Obie, "but it falls away into this bottom."

"Careful, it's wet here," warned the agent, as they continued down the bottom.

Stepping across a shallow creek, they found themselves in a cloud of gnats.

"Whew!" exclaimed Lucy, waving her hands and shaking her head. "Bugs! I can't stand this!"

"Come on ahead," encouraged Obie, taking the lead. "They're just hovering over that marsh area." As they walked up the next hill, the air cleared of the tiny pests. Obie Hardy looked out through the trees of the wooded area. "Here. It's high ground, gentle slope. A good site for a home!"

Lucy looked at the forest about them. "Here? It's just trees," she commented.

"Well, you can clear out down to the Corps line," explained Sheila.

"Yeah!" said Obie. "Just look at the slope of the ground, not the woods. And this timber might be worth something, too."

"Yeah. The owner thinks there is thirty to forty thousand dollars in timber on the property," Sheila remarked.

"I don't think it's that much," said Obie. "This is natural forest growth. It isn't seeded in pine."

"Well, you could get it cruised for an estimate. You could use that figure in your price negotiations," she added.

"All right. Good idea." They then walked through the forest down to the lakeshore. It was a natural, rocky bordered cove with no houses or boat docks. "I like it," he concluded.

"It's certainly away from it all," stated Lucy.

"I'll get a lumber estimate and get back to you," he told Sheila as they hiked back to the SUV.

"Good," she said.

Dale Gregory sat in the dental chair at Dr. Norman's office in Clarksville. He was a bit anxious, sitting with his ankles crossed and fidgeting with the newspaper folded in his lap, when Dr. Norman entered.

"Dale," said the dentist, greeting him. Noting his reading material, he commented, "Is that this week's *News Progress*?"

"Yeah," Dale answered.

"Anything interesting happening in the county?"

"No. Just the usual." *But if he only knew*, thought Dale.

"You just here for your routine cleaning?"

"Yeah. I try to do my part."

Dr. Norman picked up the folder from the instrument table, beside the spit sink. "Any problems with your teeth, now?"

"No. I'm doing pretty good."

"You want X-rays this time?"

"No. I'll wait till next year, if that's okay."

"Sure. All right, lean back and open."

His mouth felt clean as he approached the receptionist to check out.

"Can we schedule your six month follow-up?" she asked.

"Sure."

"How about April 11? Two o'clock?"

"That sounds fine," he responded. "Now, can I give you ten dollars today, and you bill me for the rest?" He had always paid in full for his visits before.

"You don't want to use your credit card?" she inquired.

"I didn't bring it today." It was the truth, although had he brought the dozen fragments his card had been reduced to, they would have been useless.

"That's fine," she smiled. "We'll see you in April."

"Great." He tucked the neatly folded newspaper under his arm as he left.

Judgments | 14

DALE GREGORY'S COURT DATE FINALLY arrived in late September, after he'd obtained a continuance in July. Dale had hired a lawyer who agreed to present his case for a $300 fee.

"Mr. Gregory," the judge began. "this warrant's been filed for failure to pay a debt to the Bank of America totaling $45,517 plus collection fees. Is this a debt you owe?"

"He does not, your honor," pled attorney Kenneth Malvern on Dale's behalf.

"Okay." The judge turned to the plaintiff's lawyer. "How does he owe this amount?"

"Your honor, this is the sum of credit card charges, fees, and interest from two credit cards, Visa and MasterCard, issued to Mr. Gregory. There had been no payments for four months when this warrant was filed. Here is a copy of our agreement and terms." The attorney handed the contracts to the judge.

"Mr. Gregory, these are standard credit card agreements or contracts. What is the basis you have for denying this debt?"

"Your honor," Dale's attorney said, "he had his estranged wife listed as a secondary card holder. He reports that she ran up the charges herself, and when asked to help pay, she left him. He has canceled these cards since that time."

"Are you divorced, Mr. Gregory?" the judge asked Dale.

"No, sir," he answered. "We're separated."

"So you were married when she amassed these charges?"

"Yes, your honor."

"Where is Mrs. Gregory today?"

"I don't know, your honor."

"She was notified of this court date, your honor," interjected Malvern.

"Well, Mr. Gregory, marriage is a legal partnership," said the judge. "In a partnership, one partner is 100 percent responsible for the other partner. These charges were incurred while in a marital partnership. In fact, you are still legally married now. My decision is in favor of the plaintiff. The $45,517 and costs of court are due. You have two weeks to make payment of this debt."

The verdict was sealed by a pound of the gavel. So was Dale's fate.

In October, Dr. Obie Hardy attended the 2006 training meeting for state medical examiners. He parked his Jeep in the Virginia Beach Marriott Courtyard parking lot Friday morning. The meeting hotel was on the boardwalk, a mile and a half down from Hardy's hotel, the Cavalier. Missing his daily hospital rounds made Dr. Hardy feel a bit guilty, as if he was cutting classes in school. The boardwalk activities were much more slowly paced in the off-season. The conference room's full-length glass windows boasted a grand view of the ocean, the morning sunlight still dimmed by the overcast sky. Hardy sipped on his hot coffee, imagining that beach, sunny and teeming with vacationers just two months earlier. A lone jogger passed by, clad in a green nylon hoodie, breaking the monotony of gray sky and blue-gray sea.

This ME educational conference was cosponsored by the Virginia Institute of Forensic Science and Medicine, a training and research institute founded in 1999. It had been created by a founding grant from Richmond area author Patricia Cornwell. She had found fame with her locally set murder thrillers, inspired by her work in the chief medical examiner's office. Dr. Hardy looked about the room, quenching his slim hope that he might see Cornwell attending a session, to revel in the fruits of her initiative. No such luck—just middle-aged attendees and a few lecturers.

Dr. Ann Downing, the state's chief ME, was the program coordinator. She was in her early forties, with light brown hair, shoulder length. Her manner was smooth, a bit masculine, and she spoke in a very practical style. She introduced the speakers and kept the program on schedule.

A death scene slide with a heavily tattooed body sparked Dr. Hardy's memory of the Hispanic man's arm tattoo. He recreated the picture on his notepad during the lecture and took it to Dr. Downing at the break.

"Dr. Downing," he said, approaching her.

"Yes," Downing said, reading his name tag. "Dr. Hardy, Mecklenburg County?"

"Yes. I have a question for you."

"Okay."

"Do you keep a photo file of tattoos?"

"Yes. It helps ID some bodies. Also, it helps with missing persons."

"I was wondering ... we had a car wreck fatality with an unusual tattoo. It looked kind of like this." He handed her his sketch.

"Hmm. Interesting design. Any colors?"

"No. Just black. I was wondering if it was a gang emblem or something."

"I don't know. It could be," she said. "Tell you what. I'll run it by my staff, and even the police department, and see if it rings any bells."

"Thanks," said Dr. Hardy. This might prove to be a perk of attending the ME conference.

Bruce Duffer and Wilt Morris were targeted by Sheriff Larrimore at the monthly task force meeting. He wanted to review their progress on some ongoing investigations. Some of these cases were drawing public attention, and he wanted to stay on top of things.

"Any progress on the Goode Building fire?" asked Larrimore.

"We interviewed Paul Mathis's secretary," began Detective Duffer. "She described a woman who brought in a folder that she said needed to be rushed over to the courtroom. The secretary left to deliver the folder, and the woman had access to the office for five to ten minutes. We showed the secretary some photos, and guess what?"

"What?" responded the sheriff.

"She ID'd Sandy Burton, the banker for drug dealer Laymar Richards, aka Skeeter!" stated Duffer.

"Why would she target Mathis?" asked Larrimore.

"I asked Mathis about Richards and Sandy Burton," said Wilt Morris. "He said he was reviewing evidence on Richards from an undercover agent."

"So you think this Sandy Burton was the one who planted the firebomb?" surmised Larrimore.

"Most likely," concluded Duffer.

"And interestingly, we found that munitions bunker on Josh Nichols's property," added Wilt.

"It had the ingredients for homemade napalm," explained Duffer. "Forensics found napalm in the Goode Building fire. Napalm was used extensively for fire bombing in Viet Nam."

"Nichols had experience in the Navy, and he worked with explosives, no less," said Morris.

"Is there any link between Richards and Josh Nichols?" asked the sheriff.

"Not that we know of," said Duffer. "Possibly, Richards hired Nichols to bomb the commonwealth attorney's office. Nichols had his own issues with Mathis too, from his child custody battle."

"And Nichols was found dead two weeks later. Somewhat suspicious circumstances, too. We think someone may have tampered with his insulin," added Detective Morris.

"Is there anyway we can prove that?" the sheriff inquired.

"Not a chance, but *Richards* doesn't know that," Duffer suggested. "We might bluff that we know it during questioning and fish out a confession."

"All right. Good work, you two," commended Sheriff Larrimore. He seemed pleased with his detectives, uncovering a web of crimes in Mecklenburg County. "And this Richards—doesn't he tie into the Grit and Steel operation?"

"Yes," answered Duffer. "He was the suspect who triggered the whole investigation."

Later, Bruce Duffer responded to a call from Dr. Hardy's office involving a drug issue. Nurse Lucy explained to the detective that a chronic back pain patient, Frances Jeters, was requesting extra Percocet tablets.

"She told us the car ran over her Percocet pills," Lucy began. "We asked her to bring in the bottle, and this is what she gave us." Lucy handed him a tan, plastic bottle with the label torn off. It was crushed somewhat and had pill fragments inside it. "This isn't even a prescription bottle, and only half of the pills are even damaged."

"Yeah. I can see," said Duffer, examining the bottle. "I'll have this tested and see what these pills are."

"They don't look like Percocets," stated Lucy. "They look like vitamins or something."

"So this would be prescription drug fraud. I may need the DEA to get involved."

Dr. Hardy emerged from an exam room and spotted Detective Duffer. "Hey, Bruce," he greeted. "Are you here about the Percocets?"

"Yeah. It's suspicious for fraud. I'm not surprised. We've had dealings with her before."

"I'm sure you have. Oh, by the way, I asked the chief medical examiner about that bird tattoo on the Mexican in the car wreck."

"Oh, yeah?"

"Seems it is a roadrunner with a snake. The letters under it, 'eMe,' are an abbreviation for the Mexican mafia."

"No kidding? In Virginia?"

"Yeah. It's the Spanish pronunciation for the letter M, 'a-may,' for Mexican mafia."

"Mexican mafia. Wonder what he was doing here?" asked Duffer, thinking aloud.

"I don't know. It seems weird, 'though."

"I'll bounce it around and see if anything comes up. Okay?"

"Sure."

"And," he said, turning to Lucy, "I'll run with this drug issue on Jeters."

"Thanks," said Lucy. "Do you think we've got mafia around here?"

"I'm not sure," answered Duffer, thinking about the cockfights, "but I'm gonna check it out."

Dale Gregory drove over to his parents' house. He had called ahead to assure his father was home. There was a solemnity to Dale's voice telling Mr. Gregory that this wasn't just a social visit. He greeted his parents with hugs, kissing his mother's cheek.

"Mom, I need to talk to Dad about some business stuff. Do you mind?"

"Of course not," she said. "I'll be in the kitchen. I love you, son."

"Love you, too." He retreated to the front porch with his father.

"Dale," said Mr. Gregory. "How are you doing?"

"Okay, I guess." Dale forced a weak smile. "I'm dealing with some deep shit now."

"Yeah. I know some of it. I'm sorry, son." He squeezed his son's shoulders empathetically.

"Thanks, Dad." He sighed and then continued, slowly. "I don't know what all might happen. Sarina, the money, the court, my business," he said, shaking his head.

"Well, I'm here for you. Let me know what I can do, son."

"Thanks. That's why I'm here now. I've written down some things, information on my accounts, some business details. I talked to Kenneth Malvern about this stuff, too. Some of these things will seem weird, but trust me; I have good reasons for them." He handed a full-sized manila envelope to his father. "Hang on to this, just in case things take a turn for the worse."

Dale's manner was grave and his predicament foreboding. Mr. Gregory reached out to him. "Dale, you'll get through this all right. We'll pull everything together!"

"Yeah. I hope so." He gave his father a full embrace. "God bless you, Dad."

"You, too, son."

"Good-bye. I love you," Dale said, turning to walk away.

"I love you, too," responded Mr. Gregory. He stood alone on the front stoop, holding the precious envelope in his hand, helpless to shelter his son from the ominous storm that was brewing.

Ashes | 15

THE THOUGHT OF THE MEXICAN mafia in Mecklenburg County intrigued and worried Detective Duffer. He sat at his square metal desk in the open office area shared by the county investigators. At his PC, he googled "Mexican mafia." He learned that the organization had arisen in California from a Los Angeles street gang. Composed entirely of Mexican Americans, it proliferated in the California prisons in the 1950s. The group was notoriously violent, and requirements for joining included denouncing God and Christianity. Their tattoos often contained numbers, sometimes Roman numerals that correlated with their rank. The number one was for a general, with lower ranks displaying twos, threes, and so on. Except for Miami, the Mexican mafia was a rarity on the East Coast. Duffer wondered what could have drawn this element to rural Virginia.

"Grit and Steel," he mumbled to himself in response to his silent question.

Duffer shared his findings with Sheriff Larrimore at the next monthly task force meeting.

"Well," responded the sheriff, "we knew there were Hispanics involved in Grit and Steel, probably some illegals. With gambling and drugs, it's not surprising that organized crime might move in."

"This group is bad news, big time!" said Duffer.

"So, are we thinking Kevlar vests?" posed Wilt Morris.

"Yes," Larrimore stated. "Body armor would be the safest choice. How many vests do we have issued?"

"Twenty-five, I believe," answered Duffer, although he was certain of the number. They were now standard-issue equipment.

"Good. We'll need them for the bust."

Dr. Hardy and Lucy arrived at the courthouse for their day in "dog court." Obie Hardy had copied the town ordinance on leash regulations and found that the fine for violations was twenty-five dollars or more. It didn't seem to justify hiring legal counsel. Because this was his first offense, he planned to throw himself to the mercy of the court, hoping for the minimal fine. After all, he was a lifelong resident of Boydton and had owned dogs there all of his life. People from large cities—"urbanites," as one of his teachers had named them—moved to rural communities and then tried to run them like a metropolis. The leash law was an example of such imposition.

"Sarah Gauldin and Obie Hardy," the judge called out.

Obie and Lucy stepped up to the right table, Mayor Gauldin and Sarah to the left. Sarah had graying blonde hair, neatly set, with finely toned makeup. She wore business attire.

"In my past eight years as a county judge, this is the first case I've had over a town ordinance," the judge said.

Obie felt a bit of optimism, hoping that the judge might think this matter belittled his time.

"In fact, the book I have on Boydton town ordinances is dated 1972. I tried to look up this law, but unfortunately, I don't have a copy," the judge said, looking toward Mrs. Gauldin.

"Your honor," interjected Dr. Hardy, "I have a copy of the ordinance you may have, if you like." He pulled the paper from his folder.

"Sure. That would be great." The judge studied the single page for a few quiet moments before speaking again. "Obie Hardy, you've been charged with violating the town ordinance by failing to keep your dog restrained. How do you plead?"

"Guilty, your honor," he responded.

"Sarah Gauldin, do you have a statement?" he asked.

"Yes, your honor. I was in front of the pharmacy and saw the Hardys' dog running toward a mother and her child on the sidewalk. I was afraid the dog would attack the child, so I called out his name."

"The dog's name?" he asked.

"Yes. We know the dog. He's been loose in town before. Anyway, he ran toward me and was attacking. He accosted my leg with his claws. I jumped in my car to escape. I was shaking all over!"

The judge paused, pensively. "So, Mrs. Gauldin, you called this dog to you by name. Then he ran over to you and put his paws on your leg."

"Yes, your honor. He did."

"He didn't growl at you or bite you?"

"Well, no. But he was barking!"

"But isn't that what dogs do? You call them; they run up and jump on your leg. Why do you feel like he 'attacked' you?"

"I don't know, but I wasn't going to stand there and see what he'd do!"

"All right. Well, Dr. Hardy has pled guilty to the leash charge. Court imposes the twenty-five-dollar fine." The gavel sealed the judgment.

As they left the courthouse, Lucy looked at Obie with a smirk. "So you rearranged your day for twenty-five dollars?"

"Yeah. But it was worth every penny to see Sarah Gauldin making a mountain out of a mole hill!"

"Those stupid transplants!" she said. "They move here to get out of the city but then try to make this a city."

"Oh, by the way, I told Sheila about the timber estimate we got on that lake property. The seller thought there was fifty thousand dollars' worth of timber there."

"Yeah. And the company you hired to assess it estimated eight to ten thousand. Right?"

"Yeah. I was hoping they would lower their selling price, but, instead, they cut the timber themselves and kept the same price. They're saying the property is improved now because it's more 'open.'"

"What? Improved? You're kidding."

"Anyway, we haven't made a deal yet. I guess we'll keep looking."

In October, the two-week deadline for Dale Gregory had expired. He returned to the court room on Friday, the thirteenth. He came alone, his estranged wife not to be found and his lawyer unaware of his plan of action.

"Mr. Gregory," began the judge, peering over his reading glasses, "it seems that you have not begun payments on this debt. Do you have the money to pay on this now?"

"No, your honor, I do not."

"Why have you not complied with my court order?"

"I've been … unable to reach my wife, and … I don't have the assets to make any payments yet. Maybe … if I had some more time …"

"You had been billed for months before, and this case was continued to give you more time, and you've had an additional two weeks to arrange payments. So far, you've not paid a cent! You've violated a court order now. I'll now have to sentence you to six months' imprisonment."

"But your honor, I won't be able to pay anything if I can't work!" pleaded a desperate Dale.

"Your sentence starts today. We'll evaluate you Monday for work release program eligibility. You may go and ready your affairs and report to the Mecklenburg County jail by 7:00 p.m. today." Thus dictated the law.

Bruce Duffer had just finished dinner when he received a call from the sheriff's office.

"We have a suspicious fire in Buffalo Junction. And there's a body inside."

"Okay. Has the coroner been called?" he asked.

"No. We'll call for one now," stated the dispatcher.

"Okay. I'll be there in twenty minutes." He hung up the phone and turned to his wife. "So it is Friday the thirteenth after all. A burned body in a house fire in Buffalo Junction."

"Oh, darn it," responded his wife. She would be abandoned but was aware that he thrived on fire investigations and that the county needed his expertise. A death scene would make it even more complicated. "Oh, well hang on to your glasses this time," she said.

"Thanks," he said, smiling.

The 9-1-1 call for the Clarksville Volunteer Fire Department had come at 7:00 p.m. A resident of Buffalo Junction had reported a neighbor's house was on fire. The trucks rushed to the address to find the house engulfed in flames. The driveway ran alongside the building to the back, so the trucks had approached the blaze from the rear of the home. A white pickup truck parked out front led the fire fighters to assume the building may be occupied. They immediately charged their hoses and attacked the inferno.

The detective found the fire chief promptly upon his arrival. Another fireman showed Duffer a photo of what the scene had looked like when they first arrived. The fire was largest in the center of the house. Because the origin of the fire often produced the biggest blaze, Duffer knew he would need to focus his efforts there first.

"Who called this in?" he asked the chief.

"Supposedly, a neighbor saw the fire." The chief motioned toward homes across the street from the front of the house. "About nineteen hundred, seven o'clock."

"Was the house locked?"

"The front and side doors were, but the back door was burned through. We entered there."

The building was a small, narrow three-bedroom house with a brick veneer exterior. A chimney was in the rear, marking the den fireplace. The smell of the burned house was flavored with a trace of scorched flesh. Duffer, wearing his work boots, entered the back doorway. The door was burned and broken, but he found the latch hardware. The dead bolt was protruding, indicating that this door had been locked as well. He was directed by the fire chief to the bedroom to his right. The mound of ashes beneath his boots was a soggy, black mud from which smoldering gray smoke still rose. Half buried in the cinders, the body was visible on the bedroom floor.

Dr. Hardy had been summoned as the medical examiner and arrived at the house fire location at 8:50 p.m. He parked out front, avoiding the traffic jam of emergency response vehicles along the side and back. Duffer had emerged from the ruins and stood by his Crown Victoria sedan, opening the trunk.

"Hey, Doc," Duffer said. "Happy Friday the thirteenth."

"Yeah," responded Hardy, dryly.

"This is a suspicious house fire, called in at seven o'clock. There's a body, presumed to be the owner, in the back bedroom." He removed his camera and a box-shaped device from his tool trunk.

"Whose house is it?" Dr. Hardy asked.

"Dale Gregory. Oddly enough, he was at the courthouse this afternoon and was due to be locked up tonight. Something about some big money and a nasty divorce."

They walked across the steaming debris to the bedroom remnant, Duffer in boots and Hardy in street shoes. Hardy watched his own shoes as he stepped onto the soggy soot and just shook his head. He found the man's body amongst the bedroom cinders. The brown, roasted buttocks and portions of the thighs were the most recognizable anatomy. The head was a blackened, ball-shaped mass, not unlike a giant match stick head. Sooty rubble largely covered the limbs. Dr. Hardy donned his exam gloves to touch the corpse as Detective Duffer began flashing crime scene photos. The leathery skin was still warm, stiffened by the cooking of muscle tissue. The outermost portions of the forearms and hands were largely buried, as were the knees and mid lower extremities. There was little remaining of the feet still visible in the ashes.

"This one is for Richmond," stated Hardy. There could be no fingerprints and, depending on the tissue integrity deep in the gluteal area, questionable useful DNA. "They will need to do a definitive ID and determine a cause of death. This could be accidental, suicide, or homicide."

Detective Duffer placed the probe from his box instrument on the surface of the cinders. "Positive—that rules out accidental," he announced, eliminating one of the four causes of fires.

"What's that gadget?"

"A hydrocarbon detector. It tests for accelerants used in setting fires."

"Oh. So, it's not likely an accident, then."

"That's right. And the weather's clear. Doubt that it's lightning, unless, of course, it's *Jewish* lightning."

"What's Jewish lightning?" asked Hardy.

"That's when an owner burns down his building to collect the insurance money."

"Oh, I see. I guess he wouldn't have burned himself up in the fire if it was that."

"Unless someone burned him and the building. Then they'd collect life insurance, too."

"Like lightning striking twice!" Hardy mumbled.

"Yeah, exactly! I'll come back in the morning and sift this debris for body parts and other traces of evidence."

"Have fun," mused Hardy. "I'll fax my report to the central ME office." He turned and headed back to his Jeep.

The detective returned his equipment to his car. As he was closing the trunk, he noted two red plastic fuel containers in the backyard. He took a sniff from the spout of one. "Diesel fuel," he said aloud. That made sense, with diesel-powered construction equipment parked under the back shed. There was something dark on the ground beside the empty containers. He picked up the object—a black wool coat that appeared to be a women's style. The scene already emanated of arson, but, if this meant another person was involved, they were looking at the involvement of an accomplice or, more likely, a murder.

Questions | 16

Sarina Gregory sat in the office of Kenneth Malvern, the attorney who had represented Dale in court. Brad had accompanied her but waited, respectfully, in the reception area. She wore a tight-fitting black dress and black stockings to project a mourning facade. Dale's father sat adjacent to Sarina, facing the attorney, with a manila envelop in his lap.

"I've reviewed Dale's insurance documents and last will and testament," began Malvern.

"He made a will?" asked Sarina, astonished.

"Yes," he continued. "It is all in order, and I'll file it with the county. Unfortunately, Mrs. Gregory, he's left you the house."

"But it's burned to the ground!" she cried. "Will the insurance pay?"

"It would have, except that he let the policy lapse. He hadn't paid a premium in over six months."

Mr. Gregory remained silent and unmoved, being already aware of these facts.

"He had life insurance, too. I know. I paid the last premium myself."

"That's true. However, after you were separated, Dale changed the beneficiary to his father, Mr. Gregory. He's entitled to the $250,000 from Southern Life. The company won't pay out, however, until the police close the case and determine whether his death was accidental, suicide, or—God forbid—murder."

Mr. Gregory glared at Sarina when the attorney mentioned murder.

"Well, what's left for me?" asked Sarina, fidgeting a bit.

"Well, since you were legally married at the time, the entire court judgment debt of $45,517 falls on you. Plus my court fee that is still due."

Sarina's world had been turned upside down. She had been expecting the homeowner's insurance payment and the stepped-up life insurance claim, hundreds of thousands of dollars! She had underestimated Dale and was now left holding the bag. Her cheeks flushed with anger, her thoughts racing. *Wait*, she thought, *my uncle's a lawyer. He'll get me some money!*

"Well, then," she said, standing up indignantly. "You'll be hearing from *my* lawyer! Both of you!" She turned her heels and barged out of the office, Brad in her wake.

Mr. Gregory's composure was mildly disrupted. He shook his head side to side. "I feel like she did this to Dale," he stated. "Either she killed him, or she drove him to kill himself. She can burn in hell, for all I care!" Such strong words were uncharacteristic of this man. He had been deeply wounded by his son's senseless death.

"I knew he was in trouble," said Malvern, "but I never thought … I'll help you any way I can."

"Thanks, but what I'd really like is her behind bars!"

It had been over a week since the fire, but Detective Duffer's investigation was still ongoing. He contacted Dr. Ann Downing, the chief medical examiner, by telephone to discuss the Gregory fatality.

"Did you get those dental records I sent on Dale Gregory?" asked Duffer.

"Yes, and it's a good thing," stated Dr. Downing. "The remains were too burnt for usable DNA, mostly skeletal."

"I thought so."

"The records confirmed the body was that of Dale Gregory. No surprise. But the skull showed multiple fractures, apparently present prior to death."

"Head injury? Was that the cause of death?" the detective probed.

"Most likely. Again, the remains were so damaged that organ samples could not be examined. Were there signs of anything falling on his head in the house?"

"Possibly. The house was flattened by the fire. I'll look over the photos again and review my notes."

"I'll hold the manner of death as pending until you determine whether suicide or murder is more likely. It's rather violent and flamboyant for a suicide, though."

"Okay. Thanks." For Detective Duffer, cases never seemed to be straightforward. He had questioned Dale's friends and relatives earlier. The wife had been having an affair and had not been entirely covert about it. And there was the question of what they suspected to be her coat beside the empty diesel fuel jugs in the yard. He'd have to interrogate her more thoroughly.

Sarina was unnerved when she arrived at the police department for further questioning. Her plans had all crumbled, and now investigators' suspicious eyes were focused on her. Bruce Duffer and Wilt Morris sat across from her, a dictaphone recorder on the table.

"Mrs. Gregory," said Detective Duffer, "we're sorry to have to intrude again so soon after your loss. We just need a few more details to complete our investigation of Dale's death."

"Okay."

"Can you confirm for us, again, where you were between 6:00 and 7:00 p.m. on Friday, October 13?" continued Duffer.

"Yes. I was in South Boston."

"Where, specifically?"

"Well, I had dinner at the Molasses Grill from seven to eight thirty. Then I watched a movie on TV at the Quality Inn, where I was staying." Her speech was unencumbered, rehearsed, and consistent with her earlier statement.

"And do you have any witnesses who might verify this?" asked Detective Morris.

"Um, there were people dining at the restaurant, but after that, just Brad Wilkinson."

"He's your boyfriend, right?" added Morris.

"Yes."

"Is this your coat?" asked Duffer, holding up a black pea coat. She looked at it hesitantly, unsure of its implications.

"Well, yes. It looks like mine."

"Can you explain why we found your coat outside of the house that night?" asked Duffer.

"I guess I left it at the house when I got out in June. It hadn't turned cool then." It was a plausible explanation.

"How do you think it got out in the yard that night?" probed Morris.

"I don't know," Sarina said firmly. "I haven't seen that coat in months."

"Did you increase the amount of coverage on Dale's life insurance policy?" Duffer asked.

Sarina paused before answering. "Yes."

"Why?"

"I thought that I … I mean, *we* might need more, you know, since we had some credit card debt … equipment loans." She realized how this sounded.

"Doesn't your boyfriend sell insurance?" continued Duffer.

"Yes. He does."

"Were you expecting Dale to die?" injected Morris.

"Absolutely not!" she stressed.

Duffer and Morris exchanged discriminating glances. "We'll need to talk to Brad Wilkinson, of course, to confirm your alibi," concluded Morris.

"Okay." A wave of uncertainty passed over her. Brad had been reluctant to be involved in her scheme from the start. She needed his absolute faithfulness to shield her from further scrutiny.

The following day the investigators brought Brad Wilkinson in for questioning. He was escorted to the same room Sarina had visited. There was a scent of burnt coffee and stale cigarettes staining the air, smothering any levity. Brad had been briefed by his partner about the process and coached on possible questions.

"Mr. Wilkinson, I'm Detective Duffer, and this is Detective Morris," said Duffer.

"All right," said Brad, nodding.

"We need to have you clarify some details for us regarding Dale Gregory's death."

"Okay."

"Did you know Dale Gregory?"

"Not directly. I knew of him and some about him from his wife, Sarina."

"She's your girlfriend, right?" continued Duffer.

"Yes," he answered.

"How long have you been seeing Sarina?" inquired Detective Morris, with a bad-cop air.

"A little over a year, I guess."

"And did you know she was married when you started dating?" asked Morris.

"Yes. But she was planning on leaving him." He proceeded to confirm Sarina's alibi, nearly word for word.

"Mr. Wilkinson," said Duffer, "what do you do for a living?"

"I'm an insurance agent."

"Did you know Sarina recently increased the life insurance on Dale?" interjected Morris.

"Ah, yes. She told me," he admitted, softly.

"Had you *advised* her to do this?"

"No! That was her idea!" he blurted, unintentionally implicating his mate.

The detectives shared a stern look. "Did Sarina plan to kill her husband?" Morris asked directly.

Brad appeared more anxious, his face flushing and his hands quivering. His discomfort was obvious. "I do not know of any such plan," he stated cautiously.

The officers looked at each other again, their suspicions aroused by his choice of words. "Mr. Wilkinson," Duffer said and then paused. "Did you receive a cell phone call from Dale Gregory's phone at 6:58 p.m. on Friday, October 13?" He laid a Verizon telephone log printout on the table before Brad.

Brad saw that his number at the bottom of the printout. "I … I didn't answer that call. He must have called me when Sarina wouldn't answer his calls, trying to reach her," he hypothesized.

"We found his cell phone in Sarina's coat pocket, outside the house," announced Duffer.

Brad Wilkinson had been unable to respond to the officers' revelation about where they'd found the cell phone. His composure had visibly deteriorated as his nervous system was bathed in adrenaline. After letting him simmer a while, the officers excused him. Following his departure, Duffer remarked, "Did you notice the time of the phone call? 6:58?"

"Yeah," answered Morris.

"It's twenty minutes after the fire was started. That fact I didn't share with him. It may be significant evidence."

"I'd say so. This thing reeks, and that Sarina is bad news." The officers shared the same impression.

Dale's father carefully packed a ceramic vase in a box, cushioning it with plastic bubble wrap. He taped it securely before driving to the Clarksville Post Office. He was mechanically following the directions Dale had entrusted to him. Placing the package on the counter, he asked the clerk for an international zip code in Mexico. After completing the address, he paid the postage fee for the weighty item. As Dale had warned, it was strange for Mr. Gregory to fulfill this final request. Not breaking his promise to Dale, he had not told his wife the full story. He motioned the sign of the cross with his right hand, kissed his fingertips and touched them to the package.

"Would you like to insure your package?" asked the postal clerk.

"No, thank you," he said, smiling weakly. The value of this package was not monetary.

Grit and Steel | 17

It was one thirty in the afternoon at the Mecklenburg County Sheriff's office on Sunday, January 22, 2007. A light rain was falling, making the forty-eight-degree temperature feel even colder. Detective Duffer and most of the county's deputy force were mustered. Six state police officers joined the ranks of the eighteen county deputies gathered for the operation. Virginia state trooper Bob Walden stood up in front of the crowd cramped into the office building and addressed the crowd.

"Okay, men. We have three DEA agents among our state police team here today. Also, two men from Homeland Security will be identifying and processing illegal aliens. The livestock truck outside is for the Department of Agriculture and the Humane Society to impound roosters. We will write up citations at the scene and detain only felons for jailing."

"We have three county school buses," announced Sheriff Larrimore, "to hold people while we process their paperwork. We suspect a hundred or so people will be present. The Mecklenburg 'tact team' will lead the convoy to the site. Be prepared for gunfire, as we suspect some organized crime members may be involved. We hope this will run smooth and quiet."

"Okay," declared Walden. "If we're ready to go now, Operation Grit and Steel is commenced! Let's go, men!"

The caravan of county cruisers, state police cars, school buses, and an animal truck turned onto Red Lawn Road at 2:00 p.m. Despite the seven-month investigation and the amassing of an army of various departments, Operation Grit and Steel had remained covert, unsuspected by the congregation at the chicken barn.

This Sunday was a special derby event, the "Super Bowl" of cockfights, coinciding with this weekend's international World Slasher Cup in the Philippines. All serious cockers were excited about this week. There were about fifty vehicles parked in the woods and field around the cockfighting barn. Once the tactical team members had established their positions around the building, the police blasted some sirens and lit the air with flashing blue lights. The area was teeming with police as the cars continued to encircle the perimeter. The weather had played to their advantage by deterring outside loitering; most attendants were inside the building. The two doorways were secured by the tact team, but there were about fifteen visitors still in the parking area when the invasion began. They took flight, scattering as they ran across the field toward the surrounding wooded areas. Two deputies gave pursuit, but heavy work boots, wet ground, and poor physical conditioning impeded their progress.

"Halt! Police!" cried one of the officers, firing a shot at the sky to prove how serious he was. The fugitives disappeared into the underbrush around the field.

Detective Bruce Duffer had driven the first school bus to arrive, each being driven by a detective. Four deputy passengers accompanied him. With the rain-saturated ground and operating an awkward vehicle with no off-road capabilities, he had chosen to park along the edge of the entrance drive. His handheld radio began receiving broadcasts from the tactical team, now inside the premises.

"It seems there are some minors present. A few women, too," announced the tact team.

"How many minors?" responded Duffer.

"Maybe a dozen. Only five or six women."

"Okay," answered Duffer. "The first bus is number 11. Bring the women and juveniles to that bus."

"Ten-four. Women and children to bus eleven," confirmed the team.

"Let's gather any suspected illegals to the second bus," directed Sheriff Larrimore. "What number is the second bus?"

"Bus number 58," said Wilt Morris over the radio. He was driving the second bus, positioning it parallel to bus 11.

"Affirmative. We copy. Women and children to bus 11. Suspected illegals to bus 58," acknowledged the tact team member.

"Ten-four," confirmed another team member.

The deputies herded the captives, in groups of two or three, from the barn through the winter rain to the buses. Sheriff Larrimore and the state police searched the building for contraband. The concessions counter held the admission fees, as well as the sales revenues, totaling about fifteen thousand dollars. Beside the cockpit area, there was a cardboard box with thirty-two hundred dollars in fight entry fees and assorted wagers. Larrimore and Agent Walden stashed the ill-gotten cash into evidence bags and labeled the contents. Numerous small cages of roosters were stacked near the cockpit, the sounds of their feral pecking and scratching giving the barn a feeling of restlessness.

Four men dressed in gray coveralls began sorting the cocks and carrying the cages to the truck. Some had large plastic trash bags for gathering the carcasses. Most of the dead birds were in the scorched steel trash barrel, but others were strewn around the pit and outside the building. The humidity intensified the odors that filled the barn. Wet feathers, bird feces, and cigar smoke trails tainted the cool, damp air.

"Sheriff, we got 126 roosters in cages," announced a Humane Society worker. "Still counting the casualties."

"Great. Thanks," answered Sheriff Larrimore. He and Walden were continuing their search around the cockpit. "Here's some cockfighting paraphernalia," he said to Walden.

"Yeah. The gaffs, or spurs. They come in these bayonet styles," Walden said, holding up a metal leg augmentation shaped like a curved ice pick. Then he picked up another spur, more resembling a sickle. "And there's this knife, or blade, style—so the cocks can either stab or slash."

"Sort of like street fighting. We'll confiscate these as well."

The Humane Society worker showed them a medicine vial and syringe. "We found these among the cages," he said. "They look like steroids and adrenaline. It helps peak their aggression."

"Great," commented the sheriff. "What a brutal sport."

A man in a black jacket with large "DEA" lettering across his back approached Larrimore and Walden. "It's truly a drug den here," he stated. "We've found marijuana, cocaine, and some narcotics. One person had the biggest stash, though."

"That would be Laymar Richards," noted the sheriff.

"That's right! You got evidence on him, already?"

"Yeah. Plenty! His investigation led us to this bust. We're investigating him regarding an arson case as well."

"All right. We'll take him in."

On bus 58, Detective Wilt Morris was processing suspected illegal immigrants. He repeated his question routine. "Name and ID?"

"José Mortez," stated the next man in line, extending his driver's license with his right hand. Morris studied the license and noticed the man's prosthetic left arm.

"So you live here, José?"

"Yes."

"How long?"

"Six years."

"Did you organize this setup? The fights and all?"

"No, sir. I just take care of the building—open it, lock up, and stuff." The undercover work had revealed that he was greatly belittling his involvement.

Morris wrote continuously on his clipboard. "José Mortez, I'm warranting you for illegal cockfighting because you charged admission and promoted gambling. All monies involved will be confiscated. You are due in court on the listed date." He tore off the citation and handed it to him. Then he turned to the next man in the crowd. "Name and ID?"

"Donte Sanchez," answered the next man. He appeared Hispanic, as well, and had a nose ring and a scar on his cheek. Removing his jacket, he feigned a search for his nonexistent ID. His forearms were exposed, exhibiting a tattoo of Roman numeral IV and a serpent. Morris realized this tattoo was likely a gang emblem.

"I can't find my ID," the man said. "Maybe it's in the car."

"Mr. Snipes," said Morris, beckoning his associate. Mr. Snipes was an agent of Immigration and Customs Enforcement, or ICE, and was processing people who were in the country illegally. "This one's for you."

"All right," responded Snipes, directing Sanchez his way. This would require more than a misdemeanor citation.

"Name and ID?" continued Morris, almost mechanically.

"Chavis Tezman." It was the Tidewater farm hand.

Despite the involvement of six different agencies and the cold, rainy weather, the process neared completion in about three hours. There had been an abundance of radio chatter on the police bands. Even without broadcast of the address, this had drawn some local spectators. Red Lawn Road was not that long of a road, and the site of this commotion was obvious. Their curiosity had been rewarded.

Deputies held the onlookers behind the perimeter of the activity, preventing any interference in the operation. Mark McClain, a local reporter, spotted Sheriff Larrimore and waved enthusiastically at him. The sheriff was familiar with McClain; he was known to monitor emergency channels on his scanner, looking for a scoop. Larrimore approached him, pausing briefly from his law enforcement duties to fulfill a public service obligation.

"This raid," he announced to McClain, "is the result of coordinated efforts from multiple agencies. We've conducted a seven-month investigation, code-named Grit and Steel, that has culminated in this bust. I'll be available at my office in the morning to release a statement and a full report."

The following morning, Monday, Sheriff Larrimore held a press conference. He met with local county, Virginia, and North Carolina press representatives in the circuit courtroom. The volume of calls received requesting information had led him to relocate the meeting from his office. He distributed a printed report that he had just released to the Associated Press.

"Members of the press, I'm Mecklenburg County Sheriff Clay Larrimore. I've distributed to you a written report of our sting operation yesterday at a cockfighting site on Red Lawn Road. To summarize, this was the culmination of a seven-month investigation, code-named Grit and Steel. There were six agencies involved, including the Virginia State Police, the DEA, the Humane Society, Homeland Security, Immigration and Custom Enforcement, and our own Mecklenburg County Task Force. By breaking up this cockfighting operation, we have proved that the County of Mecklenburg and the Commonwealth of Virginia will not tolerate such organized criminal activity here! Cockfighting has been a felony in North Carolina since 2005 but is only illegal in Virginia if gambling is involved. Seventy percent of our arrests were North Carolina residents. I hope that our legislators will take note and criminalize cockfighting in our state."

Closings | 18

MECKLENBURG COUNTY COMMONWEALTH ATTORNEY PAUL Mathis met in the sheriff's office with Sheriff Larrimore and Detective Duffer. They were reviewing their most intriguing cases.

"So our Grit and Steel operation was a great success," began the sheriff.

"Yeah—145 arrests," cited Duffer. "Seven suspected Mexican mafia or MS-13 gang members. Good riddance!"

"We cleaned up the community and brought down a key drug dealer, Laymar 'Skeeter' Richards," said the sheriff proudly.

"Yeah. Richards has been indicted on drug possession, distribution, arson of the Goode Building, and contributing to the delinquency of minors," announced Paul Mathis. "We have hard evidence on him, and he'll be going away for some time. And most importantly, this fueled the passage of House Bill 655 and Senate Bill 592. Now, beginning June 30, attending any animal fights in Virginia is a felony."

"All thanks to our undercover agent, Stephens," added Duffer.

"What about Josh Nichols and his arsenal? Any ties to Richards or the Goode Building fire?" asked Larrimore.

"My gosh," said Mathis. "That was only a hunch! There is no evidence of any crime there. Smoke, but no fire. I'm sorry, boys."

Duffer looked down, shaking his head in frustration. "So his death remains by natural causes."

Sheriff Larrimore continued his reviews. "How about that case of Dale Gregory's death? The one that burned up in his house."

"We have a motive for the wife," said Duffer, "although misdirected, since Dale had changed his life insurance beneficiary. But she apparently didn't know this. Her coat was at the scene, her boyfriend's an insurance agent, and a call was made after the fire started. Dale surely couldn't have called anyone."

"Well, what evidence we have is only circumstantial," stated Mathis. "No witnesses, no fingerprints, not enough to try a murder case with."

"I agree," responded Sheriff Larrimore. "So we'll call this one a suicide. Okay?"

"All right," agreed Duffer reluctantly, shaking his head again. His intuition told him something was amuck in the case, but he couldn't substantiate it. There were just too many pieces of the puzzle missing.

"Still one mystery left," Larrimore stated, glancing down at his notepad. "The child from the park toilet. The remains are unidentified, and the case is still unsolved." The others remained silent. They had discovered no additional data or leads.

Obie Hardy and Lucy drove out of town along Taylor Ferry Road with Mickey loaded in the back of the jeep. On the corner of the acreage they had wanted to purchase, the realtor's sign now featured a "sold" marker.

"Did you just want to show me this 'sold' sign?" asked Lucy.

"Well, yeah. But not only that," Obie said, turning onto the hunter's access road. "I wanted Mickey to run." He stopped and opened the hatchback for Mickey to leap out and then continued down the dirt lane. Lucy knew they had finally closed on the property, but Obie still had a surprise ahead for her. At the end of the road, a freshly cleared track continued toward the lake.

"What's this?" said Lucy.

"It's our new driveway!" announced Obie. The bulldozer was sitting idle at the end of the passageway. They got out, and Obie, arms out like airplane wings, twirled about. "This is where our lake house will go!"

"Oh, boy! Finally!" exclaimed Lucy, except she refrained from spinning around. "We've got a road!" Mickey shared their excitement, running about unleashed and christening the trees with urine.

In a country house just outside of Mexico City, the Angelis family unwrapped a package they had just received. It was the vase Mr. Gregory had mailed. The sister of the late Ramus Angelis opened the letter that was enclosed:

I am so sorry that this has happened like this. These are the remains of our friend Ramus Angelis. He was cremated, as we had agreed, but the ashes you took back home were not his. I can't explain why there was a mix-up, and I apologize for any offense or grief this may have caused. You can be assured that these ashes are truly those of Ramus. He was a good worker and has gone beyond the call of duty. Please see that he rests peacefully and respectfully.

Most sincerely,
Dale Gregory

P.S. The first ashes you were given are probably not even human. Feel free to dispose of them as trash.

Ocean Paradise was a 300-unit condominium complex in Cancun, Mexico. It was midway along the hotel strip that extended from the mainland into the Caribbean Sea. Bright, white sandy beaches laced the shore where the tropical blue waters rolled in. An occasional gray iguana posed on the rocks along the dune border, basking in the morning sun. The resort manager was at his desk in his office, studying a new employee application.

"Well, Señor Angelis," he said, "how good is your English?"

"I actually grew up in the US," admitted the applicant. "My English is better than my Spanish."

"Very good. Most of our guests speak English. I like your manner, and you've had experience with a building contractor. You can have the maintenance position here if you want it." He offered his hand to shake, and it was accepted.

"Thank you, sir. You won't regret it." Dallas Angelis turned to exit. His hair was slightly long, over his ears and to his shoulders. He had a mustache, too. But despite these small changes in appearance, Dallas Angelis was unmistakably Dale Gregory.

But his reincarnation, however clever, was no miracle. Dale had feared that his life was truly in jeopardy, and he thought that a body might help bring about his own salvation. While Maxwell Walker, the funeral director, was meeting with the Ramus family, Dale had wheelbarrowed his frozen deer carcass into the prep room and replaced Ramus's body. He had then switched Ramus's relabeled dental records with his own during his checkup. They were then available to identify "his" body, found in the ashes of his house. At Ramus's memorial service, José Mortez had offered any assistance he could give. Dale had taken him up on it and sought help getting an alias and a passport. José had connections with a Mexican mafia source who produced the document for one thousand dollars.

With his new identity, Dallas had purchased a used car in Oxford, North Carolina, with cash money. His bank account there was then liquidated. He had placed Ramus's body in his bedroom and lit his home on fire. From his blazing house, he had hitchhiked to Oxford and then driven south on I-85.

He had left enough props to draw suspicion toward Sarina. He had extracted Brad's phone number from his cell phone company records and placed a final call from his cell phone to Brad before dropping the phone in Sarina's coat pocket. His hope was that, if given enough rope, she would hang herself. If she had been planning his murder, the scene would seem incriminating. She had totally destroyed his life, emotionally and financially. Her fate was not his concern, but feeling that he had encumbered her life and possibly alienated her lover brought him a sense of satisfaction. And a new life on the Mexican Riviera wasn't half bad either.

Preview

Planned release December 2013

ELEMENTAL DANGER

Picking Bones | 1

It was a pleasant, sunny May afternoon in rural Virginia. Since it was a Wednesday, Dr. Obie Hardy was finishing his office work early, planning to enjoy his yard and grill some hamburgers. For over two decades he had practiced family medicine in the small town of Boydton. As he dropped a final stack of office charts on the refile counter, his medical assistant, Lorene, spoke.

"The sheriff's office needs a Medical Examiner," she said.

"Great," sighed Dr. Hardy.

"They're on line one," she added.

"Dr. Hardy," he acknowledged, hitting the speaker phone button. All of his patients were gone for the day, so this discussion would still be private.

"Yes. We need an ME on route 722, Buffalo Springs area, near the Halifax County line. It's on the lake shore." The doctor realized that this was at least twenty miles one way. A typical death scene visit took him over an hour to work. It might well be dark by the time he got home.

"Okay. I'm on my way."

Dr. Hardy was one of the five doctors in Mecklenburg County who served as local medical examiners, or coroners. They worked fatality cases as extensions of the central office into their rural community, a hundred miles from Richmond. Local MEs receive a small per case stipend for collecting the necessary information and body fluid specimens, if needed. He grabbed his nylon ME bag, stocked with state forms and collection supplies, and headed west on highway fifty-eight.

The tortuous drive down back roads took him past Buffalo Springs to a somewhat geographically isolated region along the southern banks of Buggs Island Lake. A Mecklenburg County police cruiser parked beside a cabin marked the site for Dr. Hardy.

An overweight, uniformed deputy met Dr. Hardy at the cabin. "Dr. Hardy. I'll take you from here to the scene. It's a couple hundred yards back this way," he indicated. He led Hardy along a steep path down from a bluff behind the cabin. The vivid blue water spread out below them, soft mounds of white clouds rolled slowly through the sky above. There was a bridge visible far down the lake and Dr. Hardy realized it was the train trestle at Clarksville, at least five miles away.

The path ended on a beach of tan colored sand with four to eight foot tall brushy trees scattered about.

"There's Detective Duffer over there," pointed the deputy, sounding a little winded.

"Thanks."

Bruce Duffer was a few years younger than Hardy, probably about fifty. This capable Mecklenburg County detective was seasoned by twenty years of experience. He was about six feet tall, brown hair, wearing a dress type shirt and khakis. He looked over at Hardy.

"Dr. Hardy. We found these remains over here." Hardy approached cautiously, expecting a water logged corpse, wet and decayed. "The remains are all skeletal," he announced, gesturing toward the wooded area up the beach. "We've marked and photographed the bones up front. You can check those first."

Hardy walked towards the first marker where he found a large bone.

He identified it as a left femur (thigh) bone. He marveled at the pristine condition of the bone, a welcomed change from the fetid, rotting bodies often encountered by MEs. Detective Duffer had brought him a large, brown paper bag, like a shopping bag.

"Left femur," he announced, carefully depositing it into the bag. The bone was white and dry, no adherent organic material remained. The next skeletal element marked was the pelvis. It was completely intact. The osseous ring demonstrated an unmistakably masculine contour. "This is a male," concluded Dr. Hardy.

"Are you sure?" probed the overweight deputy, Johnson.

"Yeah," he said. "Definitely."

"Well, there's a female missing person from Halifax County. She's been lost about three months. People said she was kinda manly, not very feminine. Could this be her?"

"No, it's a male pelvis," remarked Hardy. "And, besides, these bones have been here over six months." The sand, sun, and weather had cleaned and bleached this skeleton to the quality of an anatomic teaching model.

"Any idea on how old he was?" asked Duffer. Hardy had just harvested another bone sample, a portion of the lumbar spine. Five vertebrae were fused with calcified, hardened growth connecting them. This was an arthritic process that would not be seen in a young adult.

"Over thirty," stated Hardy. "Probably age fifty to sixty." The osteoporosis seen with more advanced ages was not present. As they proceeded inland to the woods, the bones were more scattered -- a couple of hand bones, some ribs, a clavicle, and so on. Dr. Hardy was losing tract of which bones had been recovered. "Bruce," he said, noting him holding additional bags. "Can we sort the bags for different body parts?"

"Sure. How many do you need?"

"Upper extremities, lower extremities, spine and pelvis, ribs and head. Four or five, I guess."

"No problem. Just tell me how you want to label them."

"Okay. We'll put these vertebrae in with the pelvis. Label it 'spine and pelvis'."

Recovery became more difficult as they entered the edge of the woods. Ribs and long bones blended in with the branches and twigs on the ground, partially buried in the sandy soil and leaves. The time intervals between bone findings grew longer as the daylight waned. The dusk seemed to be falling early.

"We'll have to come back tomorrow," said Detective Duffer. "The storm's almost here!"

Dr. Hardy had been engrossed in completing the skeletal puzzle, unaware of the ominous dark clouds approaching. He now realized the wind was whipping up.

"Let's get these bones to the van," Duffer directed. He had the area yellow taped off and had methodically laid out a grid, plotting the coordinates of each bone. His arduous labor could be eradicated by a heavy storm. Dr. Hardy led the ascent along the path, followed by Deputy Johnson, carrying the bone bags, and, lastly, Detective Duffer.

The tan colored van with "Mecklenburg County Crime Scene Unit" painted on it was parked near the cottage. As Duffer was placing the bones inside, the first rain drops began falling.

"I noticed," he remarked, "there were no signs of clothing. No shoes, belt buckles, jewelry, or purse fragments. Either this person was nude or moved from the site of death. You would expect some clothing remnants to persist. You know, zippers, buttons, or something."

"Yeah. I would think so, too," responded Hardy.

"I'll come back tomorrow with a metal detector and sift the sand for trace evidence."

"Okay. I'll send my preliminary report to the Richmond office." The rain began to intensify and the group dispersed to their vehicles. Dr. Hardy called his wife on the drive home and offered to pick up pizza, the backyard barbecue having been spoiled. He could complete the CME-1 form after supper.

"That's fine," replied his wife, Lucy. "I'll make us salads and some tea."

Dinner conversation at the Hardy home often involved medical topics, since Lucy was a nurse and his office manager. Their two daughters were accustomed to this.

"So, the body was all bones?" Lucy asked.

"Yeah. Clean as an anatomy model," he stated.

"Neat," responded Anna.

"Yeah," added Vikki, the eldest. "I can't wait to tell Mr. Callahan, my Earth Science teacher." She was a high school junior but a governor's school participant. She was one of the eight students selected by her high school to spend half of each school day at the local community college. The program earned her college credits for these advanced courses. "Who do you think he was?"

"We don't know yet, but, you know, I don't mix names and tales!" He was emphatic about this. The rural community was small and healthcare data is privileged information. Occupational stories occasionally surfaced over meals as the family shared their day's events, but people were never identified. "It's still under investigation."

Boydton Life Station was the local rescue squad organization. Dr. Hardy volunteered as the Operational Medical Director, or OMD. He had been urged to attend this week's meeting as they were desperately seeking to replace their twenty year old facility. Alan Hancock, the squad captain, presided over the meeting. He was tall, with reddish brown hair and a mustache.

"Ya'll know we've used this building since 1987 when we started up. Even back then, it was a used double wide that was graciously donated." The squad initially formed with only six members, as a satellite of the well established Chase City squad. Independent after the first two years, it now boasted twelve active members and was experiencing growing pains. "First Citizens Bank has approved a construction loan for us of four hundred eighty thousand. We need to find a contractor and then make plans for a temporary base of operations until the construction is done. Anybody know a good contractor around here?"

"Shouldn't we put it up for bids," noted Mr. McClain, a middle aged, black squad member.

"I think that would be wise," noted Dr. Hardy. "I just got one estimate on my house and it's been a nightmare!" His residential construction was two months over the planned completion date with no definite end in sight. "Be sure to get a deadline with penalties in the contract."

"Who's your contractor, Dr. Hardy?" asked Alan.

"Greg Jackson. He's distant kin, like a step cousin in-law. Be wary of him."

"So, he's ass hole kin, as we say," Alan added, wryly.

"Yeah. Exactly!"

"We can run a newspaper ad and get some bids," continued Hancock.

"I can get Mark to put it in," offered Mr. McClain. His son, Mark McClain, worked as a reporter for the *News Progress*, one of the county newspapers. Mark had volunteered with Boydton Life Station for several years in the past as an EMT -- Emergency Medical Technician.

"Great," responded Hancock. "We can put Mark to work, since he don't ride calls with us anymore."

Mark McClain was a lanky black man, standing six feet five, thirty six years old. In addition to emergency training, he had studied business and communications at J. Sergeant Reynolds Community College in Richmond. He was pleased to write the Boydton Life Station ad, the request for bids, for his paper. Indeed, he submitted it as a size upgrade from the category purchased by the squad. It was just a small community service contribution by him. He was, also, working up a full page ad layout for the opponents of the "Ethanol Plant" in Chase City. This proposed plant was bread and butter for the newspaper as both proponents and antagonists bought ads to air their views.

Obie Hardy drove out to the construction site of his future home to meet with his contractor, Greg Jackson. It was on a secluded, wooded lot, one half mile from the paved road. Although off the beaten path, its saving grace was its lakeside location. Hardy noted, as he approached the lot, that the massive columns for the front porch were still lying on the ground. With only pine wood boards propping up the porch roof, the colonial style brick house lacked its potential glory. It was but one of the unfinished tasks that plagued the slothering project.

Greg sat on the tailgate of his white pickup truck. He was forty-seven years, had black hair peppered with gray, and a mustache. His tee shirt didn't mask his beer gut belly from notice.

"I thought you said you'd put up the columns last week," began Hardy.

"Well, my helpers quit on me," explained Gregg. "I've got ads out for replacements."

"I paid for those columns four months ago! They've just been lying on the ground! I could've saved a lot in interest if you had waited and ordered when you were ready for them."

"Well, the brick layers didn't work for six weeks. I couldn't put them up until they were finished."

Hardy paused. His construction loan interest was costing him one hundred fifty dollars per day. The bank had extended the twelve month construction loan for three months that would end in four weeks. His mortgage company wouldn't assume the debt until a certificate of occupancy was issued. This festering construction process was rapidly coming to a head.

"When is your expected completion date?" Obie asked flatly, still maintaining his composure.

"I guess another four to six weeks." This was the third month he had given this "four to six weeks" prediction.

"My loan runs out in four weeks. I've already had to get an extension. This is gonna be tight!"

"Oh. Here's the bill for April," added Greg, handing Obie the all too familiar manila envelope. Obie sensed that, hidden by the mustache, he was smirking.

"Well, the bank says the next draw will be the final payment. I'll turn this in but they'll hold it until the 'four to six weeks' completion date." A short silence ensued.

"Do you not want me to work anymore?" asked Greg.

"I just want the job done!" Obie Hardy exclaimed. At this point, he didn't care who finished the project.

"All right," agreed Greg.

Hardy carried his manila envelope off, walking to the house to survey the progress. Greg pulled a beer out of his cooler to drink on the long drive out the driveway and started up his truck.